Mistletoe

Magic

and Other Holiday Tales
by Nancy Christie

MISTLETOE MAGIC

Copyright © 2023 Nancy Christie

All Rights Reserved

Published by Unsolicited Press

Printed in the United States of America

First Edition

Attention schools, libraries, and businesses: this title can be ordered through Ingram. For special sales, email sales@unsolicitedpress.com.

For information contact:

Unsolicited Press

Portland, Oregon

www.unsolicitedpress.com

orders@unsolicitedpress.com

619-354-8005

Cover Design: Kathryn Gerhardt

Editor: S.R. Stewart

ISBN: 978-1-956692-65-5

Acknowledgements

"12 Days Before Christmas" originally appeared in the *Bethlehem Writers Roundtable*

"Lucinda and the Christmas List" originally appeared in *Peripheral Visions and Other Stories* (Unsolicited Press)

"The Snow Globe" originally appeared in *The Saturday Evening Post*

Table of Contents

Lucinda and the Christmas List

"Is this... No, may I speak with the... No, that's not right either... Hello, my name is...."

"May I help you?" I interrupted her, certain that, wherever this obviously scripted conversation was going, I didn't want to follow. I was tired. I was hungry. And my microwave bell was signaling that my "honey-dipped chicken tenders with fragrant mashed potatoes and crisp green beans" were ready for consumption, if not quite living up to the package hype.

But then, I thought to myself as I pulled out the tray, few things do in this world.

"I'm sorry," and then came a belch of such significant proportions that I instinctively moved the phone from my ear, in case any of the breath made its way through the phone wires.

"I'm sorry," she said again. "My name is Lucinda and this is really my first day on the job and even though I went through a lot of training—six months starting last July!—I don't think practice is the same as real life, know what I mean?"

"May I help you?" I said again, rummaging through the drawer for a clean fork or spoon. Obviously I needed to wash dishes since all twenty-three of my mismatched eating utensils were at that moment sitting in the sink with dried bits of food stuck all over them.

"Anyway, I'm calling to ask you if you have made your Christmas list yet because—"

"Look, please take my name and number off your list. I already gave at the office."

This was a lie in more ways than one. For one thing, I hadn't given anything anywhere yet—not a dime into the red kettles, not a dollar into the food pantry collection baskets. It wasn't that I was selfish or cheap or uncaring but because I just hadn't gotten around to it yet.

I'd do it as soon as I had a few extra bucks, I would tell myself every time I passed by one of the opportunities to "give so everyone can have a Merry Christmas," as one of the signs proclaimed. It was just that, so far, I didn't have any hard currency to spare.

As for the "office" part—that was just a repurposed utility closet off my kitchen where I managed to eke out a living editing theses and manuscripts and résumés for people who needed my creative touch and ability to identify the proper usage of the possessive and plural form of nouns. And the only money I had "donated" thus far was the monthly rent check to my landlord.

"I'm not asking for anything," she said, her chipper voice starting to grate on me. "Well, that's not true. I *am* asking for something but what I am asking for is your *list*. Your *Christmas* list. According to our records, you haven't submitted one yet and if we don't get it in time, there's a chance that your delivery will be delayed. After all, it *is* December 23rd."

"Oh, for—look, I don't know *who* you are or *what* you want but my dinner is waiting for me," I said, opening another drawer in search of any plasticware that would work in a pinch. I was hungry and my meal, such as it was, was starting to cool.

"Third drawer down," she said, and without thinking I moved to open the one she had suggested and then stopped in mid-pull.

"What?" not sure if I had heard her right.

"Third drawer down. That's where you put the utensils you get from Mama Leonie's and Pho Ho takeaway. Papa's Pizzeria only gives you napkins. I guess they figure you eat your cheese-and-broccoli pizza with your hands, so why waste the inventory?"

That was more than a little weird. How did *she* know where I ordered my meals? Was this yet another indication of personal information being sold to the highest bidder, namely the telemarketing industry? Or was I being *spied* on?

I instinctively closed the blinds over the kitchen sink, went to the living room where I pulled the curtains shut and then checked to make sure my front door was still triple-locked.

"I'm sorry, I'm doing this all wrong. My instructor told me if I wasn't careful, I'd scare people and that's just what I did. Let me try again. My name is Lucinda and—"

"What do you want?" I intended to make my voice belligerent and demanding, but instead it came out all quavery.

"We need that list," she said. "When you were a child, you were very good about putting it together early enough that we could access it, even if most of the items you requested weren't really within our power. And we really felt bad about that, especially the one for a real horse. That was on your list every year from when you were five until you were ten. But we did bring you the Suzy doll and her pony Sassy—remember?"

This was beyond weird and into the scary category—the stuff nightmares were made of. How did she know about *that*?

"Don't worry about how I know all this," she said reassuringly. "It's just part of your file. I mean, if I wanted to, I could even tell you what you wanted during those horrible high school years when all you asked for was—"

"A face with no breakouts and a date with Billy. And I didn't get either one," I added bitterly. "Fat lot of good writing letters to Santa did me!"

"Now, don't feel that way. Besides, that's all in the past. This is a new Christmas, and you still have time to write your list and check it twice so my boss can review it and bring you what you most need this holiday."

Just for a minute, I let myself fantasize what I would ask Santa for this year—that is, if Santa really did exist and if there was a chance that he was delivering presents to grown-up people who ought to know better than to have expectations.

How about some cash? Not a lot, mind you. I mean, I wouldn't ask to be the sole winner of the mega-million Powerball. Just enough so I could feel rich—even if it only lasted until I paid my bills and was broke again.

Or somebody to have a holiday dinner with. When I was a kid, the entire extended family—aunts and uncles, cousins and grandparents—came to our house for Christmas Eve. We stuffed our faces with way too much of my Aunt Carol's breaded chicken and ate way too many of my mother's spicy gingerbread cookies before heading off to midnight Mass where Grandpa usually nodded off and my grandmother had to keep nudging him so he wouldn't snore.

But that was a long time ago, and eventually members of the older generation died and we cousins scattered from our Midwestern birthplace to the rest of the world, settling for staying in touch via the annual Christmas emails.

I had moved to an apartment in the city, where it was just me and my computer. And most of the time I didn't mind living alone. But every December, when the grocers had signs advertising "Buy now for your holiday dinner!" and the bakery down the street advised people to "Get your order in now for your family's treats!" I found myself remembering those gingerbread cookies and wishing I had someone to share the Christmas Eve dinner with, even if the food was only takeout.

What else? Wasn't I supposed to come up with *three* wishes?

"No, that's for a genie. I'm not a genie. I'm one of Santa's elves." Lucinda's voice interrupted my thoughts and brought me back to reality. "Now, I won't keep you any longer, but if you could put something together by tonight, we might still be able to deliver on time. So have a good evening and we look forward to receiving your information." And before I could ask anything or say anything, the line clicked and Lucinda was gone.

11

I checked my caller ID, but it was of no use whatsoever. I didn't know who had called—okay, she said her name was Lucinda, but I mean I didn't know what company she was with—but the amount of intel she had on me was downright spooky. I picked at the chicken, but for some reason I just wasn't hungry anymore.

I threw away the food, and then headed back to my laptop to finish the last project I had for the year: editing a badly written novel by a guy who figured he was the next best thing in the literary world. I highlighted, red-lined and commented on about every line in the hundred-thousand-word manuscript, printed it out, and then somewhere around midnight, shut down the system, too tired to think about writing one more thing.

But all night long, I tossed and turned, my sleep punctuated with dreams about Santa and elves named Lucinda and unfinished lists and unanswered requests. I woke up the next morning, stiff, crabby, and out of sorts, and not at all happy to see that a freezing rain was pelting my windows.

Great. Christmas Eve and the powers-that-be—namely Mr. Claus—didn't even have the decency to send some snow to create the right atmosphere. No, what we got was a bone-chilling mix of wet and wind—unpleasant enough if you were only looking out the window but even worse if you had to trudge seven blocks to the post office. Which was what I had to do, thick manila envelope in hand, since the would-be novelist demanded that I snail-mail my edits back to him.

By the time I got there, the line had snaked all the way out into the lobby, with people holding packages and rubber-banded holiday card envelopes—all of which they should have sent weeks ago to avoid the December 24th rush. After forty-five minutes, I was finally able to get rid of my envelope and pick up my own mail—all bills, I noticed—before heading out in the miserable weather, my hat pulled down over my forehead as far as it could go in a vain attempt to keep my sinuses from freezing.

Maybe that was why I didn't see him. Or maybe I was too busy thinking about last night's call and wondering if I should change my phone number. In any case, I ran right into the old man, and, in the process, dropped my batch of envelopes into a puddle of dirty water.

"Sorry," I said, and he answered, "That's quite all right," and quickly bent down to pick up my mail. For an old man, he was pretty spry, I thought as I reached out for my stuff. Not that I wanted the bills but still, it *was* my mail. And maybe he thought there were checks in there—monetary gifts to help me trim my non-existent Christmas tree—that he could take without my noticing.

"No, I just didn't want them to get any wetter," he said, holding them out but I stopped in mid-reach. Had I spoken my thoughts aloud? How *did* he know what I was thinking? "Now you'd better get going because you've got that list to finish. She's waiting for it, you know."

I grabbed my stuff and backed away. Was I in the middle of some Twilight Zone episode? I *knew* what list he was talking about—the same list Lucinda had brought up the night before. My Christmas list—the one I had no intention of writing.

"Merry Christmas!" he called after me but I didn't even answer, just hopped on the first bus that came by and stayed on until three stops past my street before I finally got off and trudged back home.

It's all in your head, I kept telling myself once I was inside the apartment, door triple-locked and blinds and curtains shut. There is no such thing as Santa Claus. But as I started sorting through the bills, the idea of a Christmas list kept nagging at me. And then I found it, in the midst of all the mail I didn't want: a small green invitation-sized envelope with just my first name on the outside and inside, an invitation to the 7th Street Mission for a Christmas Eve dinner at seven p.m.

Was it just my imagination or was there a faint aroma of ginger and cloves clinging to the paper?

"Don't forget to write your Christmas list!" was scrawled across the bottom, just above the signature: "Lucinda," written in green ink with a big red smiley face next to it.

I knew where the Mission was. It was eight blocks over and three blocks down, in what was considered to be a bad section of town. There was no way I was going there. Not tonight. Not any night. And especially not now, since I noticed that it had started to snow and snow *hard*—big fat flakes that promised a significant accumulation by morning.

But if I didn't, what would happen next? Another call or a message or, God forbid, a visit from Lucinda, my very own personal crazy holiday stalker? No, anything was better than sitting here, I told myself, as I headed back out into the cold. Besides, I might as well buy this week's dollar lottery ticket.

That was my sole concession to optimism, and so far, it had proved to be a waste of four quarters.

I stopped at Hank's Newspapers, paid for my ticket, and then kept walking, all the while telling myself I should go home, as people bumped into me and the snow froze on my eyelashes. But I didn't, and before I knew it, there I was, in front of the 7th Street Mission, where a bedraggled Santa in the doorway was waving in people.

I had no intention of entering, but as I turned to head back uptown, some little kid came out of nowhere, grabbed my hand, and yanked me inside.

"C'mon," he said, pulling me. "We've been waiting forever! Mommy saved you a seat just like Lucinda said to, but we thought you'd never get here! And I'm hungry!" He pushed his way through the crowd, towing me behind him like a tugboat leading a resistant barge. And before I knew what was happening, I was shoved into an old folding chair across from a woman wearing a coat that had definitely seen better days.

"Oh, good, Paul found you!" she said, smiling as though I was her long-lost buddy. "When Lucinda was leaving, she said you'd be here but I was starting to worry."

"Lucinda?" feeling as stupid as I sounded. "She was *here?*"

"Of course," the woman said, while brushing the too-long hair out of her son's face. The kid was badly in need of a haircut, I thought. And a better shirt. And possibly a lot more food, judging by the way his wrist and collarbones were sticking out. "Lucinda is always here! Now, Paul, you can go ahead and eat," and he dug into the plate of turkey and mashed potatoes and green beans as though he hadn't eaten in days.

And maybe he hadn't, I thought, but then returned to more important matters. "So she told you I was coming," I prompted, and she stopped eating her meal long enough to answer.

"Yes. She said to save a seat for you—I'm sorry, she didn't tell me your name, but she said Paul would know who you were—and that it was very important. No, that's not right— she said that you *needed* to be here. Are you—I mean, you don't have a place to stay either?"

"No, I have an apartment," I said, digging into the food that one of the volunteers had put in front of me. For a minute I felt guilty eating what was clearly intended for those people who were hungry and homeless but, what the hell, I was here and Lucinda had said I was coming so it must be all right—not even stopping to ask myself why I was willing to accept what some strange person had said. A person, by the way, that I wasn't even entirely sure existed but if she did, was pretty weird and potentially dangerous.

"How nice," and the woman looked like she meant it. "Paul and I have an apartment, too. Or at least we did, but when I lost my job at the end of November, I didn't have the rent for this month and my landlord said if I didn't pay him by tonight he was going to throw our stuff out and lock the door. That's how I ended up here. Lucinda told me that I could get a good meal here and that afterward everything would be okay. But...."

She looked down, but not before I saw the tears in her eyes. She sniffed, blew her nose, and then looked over at her son who

16

was watching her intently. "Finish your meal, sweetheart," and obediently he went back to eating, but his sidelong glances at his mother showed his concern.

"Okay, everybody," and there was Santa, sitting in an old rocking chair on the small stage. "It's time for Santa to give the kids their gifts!" A herd of squealing short people mobbed the stage while the staff tried to get them into some semblance of a line.

"Go ahead, Paul," the woman said, but he hung back, one hand holding onto his mother's chair while the other was shoved deep into his pocket, as though to keep from reaching out. The line grew shorter, the room more littered with wrapping paper and ribbons, and still Paul waited until finally he took a chance and headed to the end of the line, followed by the last lone straggler.

"He's having a hard time with the holidays this year," his mother said, her eyes following him. "His dad died this summer. He had been sick a long time but still we hoped he could get better. And since then, Paul just doesn't expect anything good to happen. Even when he had his birthday, he refused to make a wish and blow out the candle on his cupcake. He said wishes never come true anyway. And he told me just last week that Santa was stupid, that nobody believed in him and that kids like him wouldn't get anything anyway. Maybe if he gets a present he'll believe in Santa again. You have to believe in something, you know," and she turned back to look at me. "Don't you think so? I mean, sometimes, that's all you have."

I didn't know what to say since I was more in line with her son's thinking than hers. But some response was called for so I reached into my pocket, hoping to find a couple of bucks I could give her to help with her situation. It wouldn't be much—the money I had was already earmarked for bills and stuff I needed—but at least it would be something. But all I found was the lottery ticket.

"Here," and I handed it over, adding, "It's from Santa" so she wouldn't feel like a charity case, even though she was.

"Why, thank you!" and she smiled. "I don't have anything for you, though" and she started to give it back when her son returned to the table, eyes downcast and chin quivering.

"Paul, where is your present?" she asked, and he didn't look up but just swallowed before answering.

"They said that Santa's elves must have miscounted because when we got up there—me and that other boy—there was only one present left in the bag. So I remembered how Daddy always said that we should give to others so I let him have it. But I really wanted it, Mommy! How come Santa didn't make sure there was enough for both of us?" and he burst into tears.

"Oh, baby, I'm so sorry," and she pulled him close and stroked his hair.

I sat there like an idiot, wanting to say something but at a complete loss for words. So instead I looked around for something to distract them both and saw the lottery ticket she had dropped onto the table.

"Here, why don't you do the scratch-off?" I said, tapping the mother on the arm. "You never know," although I knew perfectly well that the odds on it being a winner were slim to none.

"Good idea," she said, and gently pushed her son off her shoulder, straightening his jacket and handing him a tissue to blow his nose. "What do you think, Paul?" and she held up the card, reading the directions aloud. "'Uncover three like numbers and you win the amount shown below the numbers. Uncover two like numbers and a gingerbread man symbol and you win five times that amount.' Come on, Paul, let's see if Santa has a surprise for us after all!"

He sat up and watched her movements, but I could tell that his heart wasn't in it, especially when the first two of the six Christmas ornaments she cleared weren't a match but a number two worth one dollar and a number eight worth ten.

"All we need are three that are the same or two matches and a gingerbread man," and I couldn't tell if she was saying it to him or to herself. She uncovered a third one to show a number three, followed by a fourth ornament also bearing the number three—each worth a thousand bucks.

She stopped for a minute, but Paul jiggled her arm. "Hurry up, Mommy, we have two of them already! Maybe we'll have one more three and we'll get the thousand dollars!"

But still she hesitated, and I knew what she was thinking. If the ticket *wasn't* a winner, then Paul would be disappointed again. And I cursed myself for giving them even just one second of hope when it would most likely be followed by despair.

MISTLETOE MAGIC

"You have to believe," she murmured to herself, and scratched the second-to-last ornament. But this time it was a nine, with the two-dollar symbol below the ornament.

She waited and then took a deep breath and scratched off the last ornament face. I couldn't see what it was because she had her hand over it, trying to shield Paul from one more disappointment. But his eyes were sharp and he started yelling loud enough that you could hear his voice over the din of all the other people.

"It's a gingerbread man! It's a gingerbread man! We won, Mommy, we won!"

And he was right. They had just won five grand with the ticket I bought. Five thousand dollars. I could pay a lot of bills with five thousand dollars. I could buy a new computer and still have money left over with five thousand dollars. I could go on a vacation for the first time in years with five thousand dollars.

Just for a minute, I wanted to snatch it back—tell them that it was all a mistake and that the money was mine. But I couldn't. Not when I saw how happy Paul was. Not when I saw the relief wipe out the lines etched on her face.

Oh, what the hell. It was only money.

"Are you sure?"

I realized that the woman knew what I had been thinking and was prepared to hand it back to me if I asked for it.

"Yeah, I'm sure," and I smiled. At that moment, I felt richer than I would have had I kept the ticket.

"Oh, Paul," and she grabbed her son and hugged him. "We can pay the rent and buy some food and get you books and—" she couldn't say anything more because she was crying so hard and everyone around her was coming over to find out what had happened.

"She gave it to me and it was a winning ticket!" And she pointed to me, and the people started clapping their hands and hugging me and her and Paul, and even Santa got into the act.

"She's our Christmas angel!" she said but I shook my head, uncomfortable with all the applause and accolades since after all it was just a fluke that the ticket was a winner. I mean, would I have given it to her if I had known it was worth that much money?

"Of course you would have," someone whispered in my ear, and I turned around, sure that it was Lucinda, but with all the people I couldn't see who had said it.

Then someone started singing Christmas carols and the volunteers came around with cookies and somebody else started taking pictures of the crowd, and even though it was late and I knew it was cold outside, I didn't want to leave. And then the church bells started chiming and I realized it was midnight.

"Merry Christmas!" and the mother came around the table to hug me and kiss me on the cheek. "You don't know how much your gift means to the two of us!" and she looked over at Paul, who was singing "Jingle Bells" at the top of his voice. "It's not about the money. It's about how it made Paul feel. About having hope, I mean. And that's not something you can buy, know what I mean?"

And I did. Hope and love and faith—that was all part of the holiday spirit. Not some stupid things you put on your Christmas list. And for the first time in a long time, I really felt the warmth and magic and wonder of the season.

That feeling stayed with me all the way home, and by the time I got to my apartment, I wasn't even surprised to see a tiny Christmas tree sitting in front of my door, with a red-and-green beribboned box underneath. I carried them both inside and set the tree on the table before unwrapping the package. Even before I got the lid off the box, I knew what I would find. The aroma of cinnamon, ginger and cloves was unmistakable. And there, sitting on top of the gingerbread cookies, was a photo from the night's festivities.

There I was, with Paul and his mother hugging me and the rest of the crowd gathered around as though, for that moment, we were all one big family celebrating the holiday together.

I turned it over to read the note on the back.

"Even though you didn't write it down, Santa knew what you needed this year! Merry Christmas! Love, Lucinda."

The Snow Globe

"I don't know why I am doing this," Katherine said aloud as she pulled on her heavy boots. It had snowed again last night, and the additional accumulation combined with below-freezing temperatures would make it a miserable walk to the bus stop.

She ought to stay home. She ought to wash clothes or wipe down the kitchen cabinets. Or pack away Robert's things—no, not that. She wasn't ready yet. Maybe after she finished acknowledging the sympathy cards and scheduling the Masses the more religious of her friends had requested.

That's what she ought to do. That's what she had planned for today until the phone rang while she was washing up her breakfast dishes.

"Is Mr. Tracy available?"

Although it was almost a month since Robert died, hearing someone ask for him hurt as though it had just occurred.

"No," she said, her voice uneven, then cleared her throat. "May I take a message for him?"

"This is Tom from Apple Tree Gifts calling to let him know his snow globe is in. He can get it today, but we're only open until three since it's Christmas Eve. Or we can ship it to him," and he read off their house number and street. "That's his address, correct?"

"Yes," Katherine said, although technically it wasn't. Not anymore. "No, don't send it. I'll pick it up. Where are you located?" and she noted down the information he gave her.

But now, several hours later, she was debating the wisdom of her decision. On the one hand, the bus stop was just up the street, and the ride to the store shouldn't take more than a half hour. If she left at two, she could get there and back while it was still daylight. Katherine didn't like being out in the dark. It was hard enough getting used to being alone in the house. Coming home in the winter darkness with no one there to greet her was just too much to handle.

But it still took all she had to convince herself to go. And it wasn't just the idea of going out that deterred her. Seeing the snow globe would be a painful reminder of what she had lost— whom she had lost. But it was Robert's last gift, after all. She had to retrieve it, even if, once she brought it home, she was just going to pack it away with all the others.

But despite leaving enough time for the journey, it was nearly three before Katherine reached her stop, due to all the passengers who were also out on Christmas Eve. Once she disembarked, she looked for the shop, not sure which direction to go. Katherine had never gone there before. That was Robert's task—the one concession to the holiday that Katherine had allowed after Michael died.

Before that occurred, it was Katherine who handled all the seasonal responsibilities. She wrote the cards, neatly addressing the envelopes and signing "Merry Christmas from Mr. and Mrs. Robert Tracy" inside. She decorated the three-foot artificial tree with the ornaments Michael had given them in age order: the kindergarten ones near the top followed by those from his school years below and then the ones he sent from foreign countries during his deployments: a hand-carved nutcracker from Germany, a delicate pagoda from Japan, a ceramic cityscape of Rome.

And she baked: the kugel from her mother-in-law's collection, the pfeffernusse cookies Robert ate by the handful and the cutouts that she would send to Michael along with dozens of others. By Christmas Eve, the house would smell like an old-fashioned bake shop, and every time Robert came in the door, he'd stop, take a deep breath, and say, "Smells good!" as though he hadn't been inhaling the same aromas for the past month.

But after the military chaplain came to the house that October morning, after they had brought her son's body back home, after the funeral, the idea of celebrating *anything*, especially Christmas, seemed impossible. She had left the holiday decorations in the storage room and when, a week before Christmas, Robert asked if he should set up the tree, she just shook her head, unable to speak.

That's when he started the Christmas Eve tradition, she recalled. After midnight Mass, he had given her a small box and when she opened it, she found a snow globe with a tiny house and a snowman in the front yard inside the glass orb. And when she shook it, silver glitter fell onto the roof. Every year after that he gave her another snow globe—some traditional like the tiny Christmas tree with a cardinal perched on the top, some silly like the floppy-eared beagle chewing on a red stocking. Robert would set the new one in the center of the dining room table and then arranged the others around it.

"That's number eleven," he had said last Christmas after she had unwrapped the newest one, and then he kissed her on the cheek. "Almost an even dozen."

25

Eleven snow globes, and this year it would be twelve—one for each year without Michael. And the first one without Robert.

There was no point in dwelling on that, Katherine told herself firmly. She needed to find the store and return home. Looking across the street, she caught sight of the Apple Tree Gifts sign and crossed the intersection. Once inside the store, she said to the young man behind the counter, "Someone, Tom, I think, called this morning and said my husband's order was in."

"That was me." He smiled. "Mr. Robert Tracy, right?" When she nodded, he rummaged under the counter and brought out a box, labeled with her husband's name and address.

"Here you go. It's all paid for so just sign this slip and you'll be good to go," pushing a paper across the counter.

Just for a moment, Katherine hesitated, then she signed her name on the line while he placed the box in a bag and handed it to her.

"Merry Christmas," he said, and she nodded, unable to answer, the bag as heavy as if it held all the grief she felt.

Once outside the store, she glanced at her watch. The next bus wouldn't be along for at least an hour, and it was too cold to stay outside at the stop. She'd wait in the coffee shop at the corner, she decided, heading in that direction. At least there she would be warm.

"Happy holidays and welcome to Benny's Bake Shop!" The young waitress, wearing a bright red mistletoe corsage on her uniform, came up to Katherine as soon as she entered. "I'm Janet and I'll be taking care of you! Table or booth?"

"Table, I guess," said Katherine, and followed her to one by the window.

"Coffee?" Janet asked and Katherine nodded.

"And a muffin, too—a raisin one, if you have it," Katherine added, and in just a few minutes, she was enjoying her first dessert in—how long *had* it been? For that matter, how long had it been since she was in a restaurant? Not since Robert died. Sitting alone in public surrounded by other people just emphasized that there was no one in the empty chair across from her.

Instead, she took her meals at home, sitting on the sofa instead of at the kitchen table, and watched the news—the voices filling the silence in the house.

"Like a fill-up?" and when Katherine said yes, Janet carefully poured the coffee and then set down a few extra creamers. "There you go!" and then she turned at the sound of the door opening. "I'll be back again for another top-off in a bit" before leaving to greet the new arrivals.

Katherine stirred her coffee, half-listening to the Christmas music in the background. Robert loved the holiday songs and would play them non-stop from December first until New Year's Day. His favorite was "Silent Night," but he would reserve that hymn for Christmas Eve while she unwrapped her gift.

So many things he had done to help her cope with the loss of her son, *their* son. And only now, when it was too late, she wondered what she had done for him. What comfort had she given him? Or had she been so focused on *her* pain that she had overlooked his?

Her unwelcome thoughts were interrupted by the sight of the bus pulling up to the stop.

"Oh, no!" Katherine threw a few bills on the table and hurried out the door, making it just in time. But when she reached home, she realized her package was missing.

Where was it? Had she left it on the bus? In the coffee shop? She didn't have the restaurant's phone number, and if the bag was on the bus, someone had probably taken it by now.

Robert's last gift—and she lost it. And the enormity of her loss—of all her losses—overwhelmed her. She sank into Robert's old easy chair and sobbed in a way she hadn't even when she learned her son had died in a battle half a world away, even when what her husband thought was just indigestion— "Too much pumpkin pie," he had said in the ambulance. "There's no need to go to the hospital"—turned out to be a massive heart attack.

Katherine might have wept all evening if it wasn't for the sound of her doorbell. Who could it be, she wondered, wiping her eyes. It was dark, nearly seven o'clock. A burglar? But that's silly, she told herself as she came in the front hallway. A burglar wouldn't ring the bell! And when she turned on the porch light and looked out the window, she recognized the young waitress from the coffee shop, holding a bag with the Apple Tree Gifts label.

"You left it behind," she explained when Katherine opened the door. "And when I saw your address on the sticker, I decided to drop it off on my way home so you would have it for the holiday."

"Come in, come in" and Katherine led her inside, taking the bag from her and setting it on the side table. "I really appreciate—it was so kind of you—so thoughtful" and she started crying again. What was *wrong* with her? She hated crying, especially in front of strangers. At Michael's funeral, she

28

hadn't cried. At Robert's funeral, she hadn't cried. Instead, she had stood there, stoic and stone-faced, afraid that if she let one tear escape it would turn into a flood that would drown her in grief.

"Here, don't cry" and the young woman reached into the pocket of her coat and pulled out a crumpled tissue.

Katherine took it gratefully and blew her nose. "Thank you so much—Janet, right?" and the girl nodded. "Thank you, Janet" and then looked past the girl out the window, where the gusts were whipping the falling snow into silvery whirlwinds. No car. Janet must have walked in the darkness and cold from the bus stop.

"Would you like some hot chocolate to warm you before you leave? Or maybe not. It's Christmas Eve and you must be wanting to get home to your family."

Janet shook her head. "Not really. There's no one waiting. I've been on my own since Mom died last spring. It was just the two of us—my father left when I was a baby—so this year is my first—" and she stopped, looked away, and then finished, "my first holiday by myself."

She said it very matter-of-factly, but Katherine could recognize something behind the words: the sense of loss, of hurt, of pain.

"Then you must stay. I insist." Before Janet could refuse, she relieved the girl of her coat and hat and ushered her into the living room.

"Here, take a seat," and she settled her on the sofa, "and I'll be right back" and then went into the kitchen to warm the milk for their drinks. It only took a few minutes and then she was back in the living room with two mugs. "Here you go," and she handed one to Janet, adding, "I'm sorry I don't have anything to go with it."

"No, this is fine," said Janet gratefully, taking a sip. "Oh, I nearly forgot!" and she set her mug down and reached into her backpack to pull out a small bakery box. "I noticed you liked the raisin one, but I brought a few others, too—just a little Christmas present" and she handed the white carton to Katherine.

Inside were four muffins: one with plump yellow raisins, another redolent with the aroma of cinnamon, a third topped with sliced almonds and a fourth with melting chocolate chips. That one would have been Michael's choice, Katherine thought, while Robert would have picked the almond one.

Katherine swallowed, and then smiled at the young girl. "Thank you, my dear. That was so kind of you. Now, here," and she held the box out to her, "you must have one, too," and without hesitation, Janet picked the one with chocolate bits.

Perhaps it was the act of sharing a meal or just the Christmas spirit, but soon, the two of them were talking like old friends, Janet telling her about the night classes she was taking to become a beautician, the coffee shop regulars that she knew by name, and how nice her boss was.

"He doesn't even mind if I have to leave before my shift is over to get to school on time. I hate to think I'll have to find another place to work," and when Katherine looked at her questioningly, she explained. "My landlord is raising my rent the first of the year and my salary and tips just won't cover it. And there isn't anywhere cheaper to live—not where it's safe, anyway. So, I'll need to find a better-paying job."

She took another sip of cocoa before continuing. "But I'll manage. My mother always told me to never give up, that no matter how hard things were, something good was always waiting for me just around the corner. I just have to keep looking for it."

"She sounds like she was a wonderful person," Katherine said, and Janet nodded, looking into her mug as if to find some comfort there.

"She was," she finally said softly. "I was lucky to have her," no trace of self-pity in her voice.

Was it the recognition of shared grief that led Katherine to make the offer? Or was it because it was Christmas Eve, a time for giving, and she wanted to give something to someone who, like her, had lost someone she loved? Whatever the reason, the words came before she could change her mind.

"I have a spare room and you're welcome to it," Katherine said. "It was my son's room." She nodded toward the photo of Michael in his Army uniform on the mantle. "He died twelve years ago while in the service and his room has just been empty ever since."

"But you don't even know me!" said Janet in shock. "I mean, that's awfully kind and it would be wonderful but—"

"No 'buts,'" Katherine said firmly. "If it makes you feel better, you can give me your references, but you'd be doing me a favor. The house is so big, and it would be so nice to have someone here—" and she stopped because Janet had rushed over to hug her, almost spilling her cocoa in the process.

"I don't know how to thank you and I'll pay you rent and do anything else you need me to do and—oh, this is such a wonderful surprise!" And she kissed Katherine's cheek and for a minute, Katherine was reminded of how Michael used to kiss her when he would come home on leave.

31

"Just consider it a Christmas present," Katherine said. "Now go sit down and finish your muffin while I'll make more cocoa. Maybe we can watch some television, too—I think *The Bishop's Wife* is playing."

Janet smiled. "I love that movie! My mom and I used to watch it every Christmas Eve! But wait—you haven't opened *your* Christmas present!"

She went out to the hallway, picked up the small bag from the side table, and brought it to Katherine.

"Don't you want to know what Santa brought you? Or would you rather wait until tomorrow morning?"

Katherine took the bag and suddenly could feel Robert's presence as clearly as if he were right there in the room with the two of them.

"No, I'll open it now. It's from Robert, my husband—my late husband," she said, as she took the box from the bag. "He would buy me a snow globe every year, ever since our son died. And every year on Christmas Eve, he put the others out and then give me the new one to open."

When she saw Janet look around the room, she added, "I didn't set any of them out this year. To tell the truth, I didn't do any decorating at all. You see, Robert died just a few weeks ago and I just couldn't," and for a moment, her fingers tightened on the box.

Janet reached over and gently touched her hands. "I know how hard it is," she said softly. "I didn't know how *I* was going to get through this Christmas. But being here with you—well, that has made all the difference!"

The two women looked at each other and smiled, and then Katherine squared her shoulders. "Well, let's see what he picked out for this year." She opened the box, moved the tissue paper aside and carefully lifted out the globe.

This one had a green-striped package with a large red bow on top. And unlike all the others, it was a musical one. Katherine turned the base and the strains of "Silent Night" filled the room.

They both listened in silence until the hymn ended and the globe stopped turning. Then Janet gently picked up the snow globe and looked at it, saying softly, "I wonder what's inside that package."

Katherine looked at the globe and then at the young girl, whom she would never have met if it hadn't been for Robert's gift and smiled. "I already know."

The Little Red Sock

Phew!

The little red sock was exhausted. It had taken all his energy to wriggle his way from the bottom of the cardboard box up past the pair of old blue jeans with a patch on the right knee, through the twisted bedsheet and over the stained sweatshirt to reach the top of the laundry heap.

He'd been in the box for a whole month now, ever since the janitor had pulled him out from under the last dryer in the row, and he knew what that meant. Tomorrow he'd be dumped into the trash bin along with the rest of the forgotten, unwanted, unclaimed items that had been left behind at the laundromat.

But it's not fair, he thought. *Just because I'm little it doesn't mean I'm not important or I can't do anything! I just wish someone would give me a chance!*

He looked up at the clock where the big hand was on twelve and the small hand was on four. In one hour, it would be closing time. And he knew that the chance of somebody—anybody!—coming in time to claim him was pretty low, especially on such a cold, snowy night.

And especially when the night was Christmas Eve.

But just as he had almost given up hope, the door was pushed open by a tired-looking young woman in a torn coat, carrying a basket full of dirty clothes.

34

"Hurry up, Billy!" she called over her shoulder, and then a young boy rushed in, shivering and teeth chattering.

"But, Mommy, I was looking for Santa!" he said, as she pulled the too-small red knit cap from his head and brushed the snow from his jacket. "Can't I wait outside just a little bit longer?"

"It's too cold. Here," and she pulled him over to the bench that was under the ceiling-mounted heater. "Sit here and get warmed up, and then, as soon as our clothes are done, we'll go to the Mission. They're having a special Christmas Eve dinner tonight—turkey and mashed potatoes and maybe even some cookies! My goodness!" and from high up on the counter, the little red sock watched as the mother took off the boy's shoes and stockings, and then rubbed his feet to warm them. "Your toes are almost frozen!"

She wrapped her coat around him and smoothed his brown hair back off his forehead before adding his wet socks to the pile of clothing to be washed. "Think how good they'll feel on you once they're clean and dry," she said with a smile, but the little boy didn't answer. Instead, he kept looking out the door.

"Mommy, do you think Santa will be able to find us tonight?"

"I'm not sure, Billy," she answered, after a minute. "You know, even though Santa tries to come to everybody, sometimes there are just too many children for him to reach in one night."

The little red sock saw the frown on Billy's face and could tell that he wasn't happy with the answer.

"He has all those elves, though. Don't they give him directions and stuff? I mean, that's their job, right?" and he went over to jiggle his mother's arm as she was putting what clothing

35

they had into the smallest washer, the one that took the least number of quarters. "If I hang up my stocking, he *has* to come, right? Where *is* my stocking anyway?"

Billy's mother stopped for a minute and looked up at the ceiling, almost, thought the little red sock, as though the answer was hiding up there. Then she took Billy's hand and led him back to the bench.

"Stay here. You shouldn't be running around without anything on your feet," wrapping her coat around him again. "I don't know where your stocking is. It might have been in one of the boxes that were..." and she paused before finishing, "that were lost."

"They weren't lost, Mommy," Billy said. "Those bad people took them—the ones that stole our stuff." And when she looked at him in surprise, he added, "I heard what you told the policeman when you were in the hallway. I didn't mind the rest of it, but if they took my Christmas stocking, where will Santa put my present? And all I *really* want is a baseball," he added. "Then I could keep it in my pocket, and it would be safe, and *nobody* could take it."

She closed the washer lid, dug through her pockets for enough quarters for the machine and then, once it started, came over to sit by the boy.

"If Santa doesn't come, that just means that he had other little boys and girls who didn't have anybody at all, so he went to see them instead. But you and I," and she gave Billy a hug, "well, we have each other so we'll be just fine—even if Santa *doesn't* come! Okay?"

"I guess," but the little red sock could tell that Billy didn't *really* think it was okay. And that's when he had a glimmer of an idea. The little boy needed a stocking, and the little red sock needed a place to go. If he could *just* get the boy to see him, to pick him out of the box and put him in his pocket, then they would both have what they wanted.

But how could he get the boy's attention?

And while the clothes were swirling around in the soapy water and then spinning through the rinse cycle, the little red sock considered what he could do.

Maybe if I bounced up and down on top of the pile, he would see me, but when he tried it, he kept slipping and sliding. He just wasn't strong enough to stand straight up on top of everything else in the bin.

Maybe if I make some noise—and he sucked air in through his cuff, brought it all the way down to the tip of his toe part and then blew it back out as hard as he could. But try as he might, he couldn't make a sound

He thought about hopping over the side and scooching like an inchworm to where the boy was sitting, but it was too far away, and he didn't think he would make it in time. He was just a little sock, after all.

The buzzer sounded and the little boy's mother pulled the wet clothes from the machine and put them in the dryer.

"Just twenty more minutes," she said to Billy, who, tired of sitting on the bench, had put his bare feet back into his shoes before walking up and down the aisle. "As soon as everything is dry, we can leave."

And I'll be left behind, thought the little red sock sadly. *If only he'd come over here, he'd see me and take me out of the box.*

He watched as Billy stopped at the change dispenser near the door and opened the little metal bin to check for leftover coins, but it was empty. Then the little boy moved over to the snack machine, where he pushed every button just in case a candy bar might come out.

Maybe if I think hard enough, I'll come up with an idea. And the little red sock thought and thought so hard that he was almost worn out with the effort. But nothing occurred to him and in the meantime, the little boy kept walking from the front of the room to the back, never looking up at the counter where the little red sock was waiting.

And all the while the dryer timer counted down the minutes.

Then, just as the dryer buzzed and the little boy's mother began folding the clean items and putting them back into the clothes basket, Billy came over to the box where the little red sock was. First, he pulled out the stocking cap that was sticking up in one corner, but it was dirty, so he dropped it back into the box. Then he rummaged through the other side but nothing there caught his attention.

But just as the little red sock had almost given up hope, Billy picked him up, inspected him from cuff to toe and then pushed him deep inside his pocket.

"Ready, Billy?" the little red sock heard the mother call, and the boy ran over to where his mother was waiting with her basket of clean clothes.

After that, the little red sock wasn't sure what happened. He could tell they were outside—even from inside the pocket he could feel the cold wind—and then pretty soon Billy stopped moving and the little red sock could smell turkey and hear lots of voices and knew that they must be at the Mission.

It was warm there, and the little red sock was worn out from all his exertions at the laundromat and pretty soon he fell asleep, not waking up until he heard the sound of a key in a lock.

"Thank goodness we're home," he heard Billy's mother say. "Let's get you out of those wet clothes and into your pajamas," and the little red sock felt the jeans being pulled away from the boy. He inched his way up through the mended material until he could just see over the edge of the pocket.

The little boy was tucked up on the couch, two thin blankets piled on top of him, but the little red sock could tell by the way he was shivering that he was still cold.

"Wait!" and the boy jumped up from his makeshift bed and ran over to his pants, and the little red sock could feel himself being pulled right out from the pocket.

"Where did *that* come from?" the mother asked and Billy answered, "It was in the box at the laundromat, the one where they put stuff that nobody wants anymore. So, I brought it here to be my Christmas stocking, even if it *isn't* very big," and he looked at it critically and the little red sock could tell what he was thinking, that he probably wasn't big enough to hold even a golf ball let alone a baseball. "But we don't have a place to hang it!"

Billy looked around the room, and then, shivering with cold, he climbed back on the couch to snuggle under the covers. "I know. I'll hold it," and he slipped his right hand out, his fingers firmly grasping the little red sock. "And when Santa comes, he'll see it and that's where he'll put my baseball! And maybe he'll even bring something for *you*, Mommy," he added.

"Maybe," Billy's mother answered softly, and then she turned out the single lamp in the room, until the only light that shone in the small space was from the streetlight outside the apartment window.

"Mommy, what do you want Santa to bring you?" Billy asked drowsily and his mother answered, "Just a little bit of money so I can take better care of you," but her voice was so low that the little red sock could barely hear it.

Soon Billy was fast asleep, and the little red sock could feel his fingers relaxing their hold on him. He was afraid he might fall to the floor and tried to wriggle higher on the covers, but he was tired, too. And it wasn't long before everyone in the room was fast asleep: Billy's mother in the old rocker, her coat wrapped around her for warmth, Billy huddled underneath the thin coverings, and the little red sock, barely held in Billy's grasp.

Sometime during the night, the little red sock felt himself being lifted up and away and then a strange sensation, as though he had suddenly gotten very full and heavy. He tried to see what was happening, but he was so very tired, and it was so very dark in the room. But somehow he knew that, whatever it was, it would be okay.

And then it was morning, and the little red sock woke up, still feeling not quite the same as when he went to sleep the night before. But before he could find out what had changed, Billy was awake.

The little red sock could feel the little boy's fingers reaching out to grab him and then Billy was out of bed and running over to his mother, carrying the little red sock with him.

"Mommy, Mommy, look! Santa came and he found my stocking!" and the little red sock felt himself being dropped on the mother's lap and his cuff stretched as wide as possible and suddenly that bulgy feeling was almost entirely gone, and Billy was holding a brand-new baseball that he had pulled up from inside.

"Where did you get that?" Billy's mother asked, and Billy danced around the room, tossing the ball from one hand to the other before throwing it over to his mother, who caught and then looked at it from all sides.

"Santa came! Santa came! I told you he would if I had a stocking and he did and he brought me the baseball and that's just what I wanted!" and all out of breath, Billy ran over, gave his mother a quick kiss and then, pulling the baseball from his mother's grasp, he darted away again, holding it tightly in his hand.

"It was in *this* sock?" and the mother picked up the little red sock to look more closely at it, obviously disbelieving that such a small thing could hold an item that size.

And even the little red sock wasn't sure how and when it had happened, although he did kind of remember being moved around a bit in the night.

"Yes! *That* sock!" and Billy came over and grabbed the little red sock with his free hand. Then he stopped, his fingers moving down from the cuff past the heel until it reached the toe part.

"There's still something inside" and the little red sock knew he was right because he still felt, well, if not *quite* as full as when the baseball was inside, still kind of bulgy.

"Here, Mommy, see what's there. Maybe Santa left something for you," and Billy handed it back to his mother and then stood there, waiting.

"Oh, I don't think so," she said doubtfully, but nevertheless, she slipped her thin fingers inside and all the way down.

The little red sock could feel something being pulled up and out from down in the toe part. Suddenly that stuffed feeling was gone and he was flat again.

"Oh, my goodness" he heard her say and the little red sock looked at what she holding: a thin roll of green and white paper pieces held together with a red ribbon. She undid the bow, and then started laughing and crying all at once.

"It's money!" and she held up the bills, each one with a numeral one followed by two zeroes. "Billy, it's money! Lots of money!" and she started counting: "One, two, three, four, five, six, seven, eight, nine, ten—Billy, it's a thousand dollars!"

And she looked at her son and then around the room, as though to find out who had brought the money.

But the little red sock knew and so did Billy because he just kept yelling, "Santa brought it! Santa brought it! He knew what you wanted, and he brought it to you! I knew if I had a Christmas stocking, Santa would come! And it *wasn't* too small! It was just big enough!"

And Billy and his mother were laughing and hugging, and the little red sock was squished between them. But he didn't mind because he was happy, too. They had all gotten their Christmas wishes answered: Billy's mother, Billy *and* the little red sock—all because he didn't give up.

12 Days Before Christmas

On the twelfth day before Christmas, my mother-in-law Agnes sent me an email in which she casually mentioned that they would be arriving *not* on December 21st *but* on the 17th "so we could have more time to spend with Michael and our three darling grandchildren—and you, of course."

Sometimes I dread the holidays.

On the eleventh day before Christmas, I called my cleaning woman to request that she change my appointment from the 18th to 16th. However, she told me that, while she was sympathetic to my plight, she was solidly scheduled and couldn't accommodate me.

"I'm sure your mother-in-law doesn't care whether your baseboards and doorframes are dust-free. She just wants to see you"—which demonstrated a clear lack of understanding of the primary role of a mother-in-law: to conduct an ongoing evaluation of their son's choice of spouse and find the woman wanting in one way or another.

On the tenth day before Christmas, my husband announced that, "by the way, they had to change the date of the office party—something about a roof leak at the scheduled location—so it's this Friday night. But you won't have any problem getting a sitter, right?"

Wrong, since when I called Stacey (the only sitter on the list who was still willing to watch all three kids at one time), she claimed she was already booked.

Maybe.

Or maybe it because the *last* time she watched the kids, she spent two hours taking apart the doorknob to the bathroom because Sarah (one of the aforementioned "darling grandchildren") had locked herself in there with her favorite doll that Charley had threatened to throw down the storm sewer.

The *same* sewer where *she* had thrown his autographed Major League baseball that his grandparents had given him for his last birthday.

The *same* sewer where *Jason* was now stuck in a vain attempt to retrieve said baseball. (I didn't know that you could call the fire department for those types of emergencies.)

So, I could see where my kids *could* be too much for any one person—especially since I only paid ten dollars an hour plus all the snacks the sitter could eat—at least, before Lily, our eighty-pound omnivorous Lab, could get to them.

On the ninth day before Christmas, Sarah came home from school with a sore throat and earache that led to a two-hour visit at the pediatrician followed by a one-hour wait at the pharmacy, where other parents were *also* getting their prescriptions for the annual holiday illness outbreak.

The medication (that, by the way, cost as much as a prime rib dinner) was only for the upper respiratory issue. It wouldn't do much for the intestinal virus that kicked in on the ride home.

I was never more grateful for the plastic wastebasket in the back seat as I was that afternoon.

On the eighth day before Christmas, my in-laws arrived, with two suitcases apiece plus a two-pound box of mixed chocolates that Agnes immediately opened and started handing out to the kids, promising "there are plenty here to hold you until Christmas! And even if you eat them all, Gamma will buy you more! *Gamma* knows how much you like candy!"

That veiled intimation that my mother-in-law could be relied on to give my kids their hearts' desire when their own mother failed them would have upset me except that Michael had called his parents the night before and asked if they would mind watching the kids "so Annie could go with me to my work party. You don't mind, do you, Mom?"

Of *course* she didn't mind. His mother said she would do *anything* for her darling son, and she would love to spend a few hours alone with her darling grandchildren, "so tell your wife not to worry"—the adjective "darling" noticeably absent from the third noun.

But I didn't mind either, especially since I was well aware of two little details. One, the party usually lasted until well after midnight which would stretch the "alone" time to more than just a few hours.

And two, eating high-sugar sweets would turn my already active children into hyper little bodies that she would never be able to get into their pajamas let alone their beds by their nine p.m. bedtime.

On the seventh day before Christmas, my father-in-law Pete wandered into the kitchen where I was having my first cup of coffee and offhandedly mentioned that the toilet in the guest bathroom wasn't flushing, adding, "I tried a couple of times, but nothing would go down."

Just as he finished his sentence, I heard my husband yell a few choice obscenities followed by my name. I downed my coffee, grabbed the plunger, mop and bucket from the cleaning closet and left the room, ignoring Pete's question regarding my plans for breakfast.

The rest of the day was spent waiting for the plumber, since no matter what Michael had done, he couldn't get the toilet to work, and the other one was showing signs of backing up as well. As was the kitchen sink. And the drain in the laundry room.

After the problem was finally resolved and all the floors scrubbed and sanitized, I hunted down the box of candy, desperately in need of a chocolate fix. Unfortunately, all that it held were empty wrappers. The kids (and probably my mother-in-law) had finished them off, including my favorite: raspberry cream-filled dark chocolate.

On the sixth day before Christmas, I was treated to a return visit from our plumber (whom we really should have on retainer) since now my fifteen-year-old dishwasher wasn't draining.

"You know, you really need to buy another one," he said, his voice partly muffled since his upper torso was under the sink. Unfortunately, his lower torso was fully on display, giving me more of a view of his nether regions than I would have preferred.

I wrote him the second check of the week and realized in the process that I had now exceeded my household repairs budget by about $200, thanks to the weekend service call surcharge that had been tagged on to both bills.

On the fifth day before Christmas, I received a frantic phone call from my sister who needed a pet-sitter because her husband had surprised her with a five-day cruise to the Bahamas and they were leaving the next day.

"We'll be back by the 27th. And Bad Kitty won't be any trouble, I promise," she said. "All you have to do is give him his canned food every morning by six a.m., and a scoop of dry food at supper time. Oh, yes, and don't let him near the Christmas tree or any of the presents because he likes to eat the ribbons. And the tinsel. And chew on the cords. And you'll have to give him his hairball medicine at noon, but that's easy: just catch him, hold him down, and shove a small bit into his mouth. He won't bite—not if you're fast enough, anyway."

What could I say? She was my sister. And the kids were thrilled to have Bad Kitty for a holiday visit, unlike Lily, who came over to sniff the new arrival and ended up with a row of bloody scratch marks across her muzzle.

On the fourth day before Christmas, I learned three things about Bad Kitty. One, if I gave him too much canned food, he would eat it all and then throw it up in a convenient spot—like inside my favorite pair of slippers.

Two, he wanted the litter box scooped as soon as he used it. But since I had more things to do than check on his bathroom visits, if I missed a session, he would leave me a "present" just *outside* the box. That cat poops more than anyone else in the house.

Three, he not only liked to *chew* the needles on the Christmas tree but also liked to climb the trunk. At first, he settled for going just midway up. But the last time, he apparently just couldn't resist heading all the way north. And since he weighed about eighteen pounds, when he *did* get to the top, the entire tree tipped over, dumping decorations onto the floor.

Lily ran into the room to see what the noise was and then took off with the angel from on top of the tree while Bad Kitty hid behind the couch where he threw up again.

I righted the tree, cleaned up the broken ornaments and the cat puke, and realized that now the string of two hundred lights wasn't lit. Apparently, they were the type that, when one bulb failed, they all stopped working. So now my lighted tree *wasn't.*

Not having the time or patience to do a search-and-replace for the broken bulb, I left the room to retrieve the angel (now missing one of her wings) from the dog and stuck her back on top of the tree.

On the third day before Christmas, Charley finally gave me the list that he had had in his backpack for well over two weeks, detailing items he had to bring to school before winter break started. Tomorrow. A list that included twelve dozen cookies as well as ideas for gifts for his teacher, cafeteria monitor, bus driver and a classmate for whom he was a "Secret Santa."

Fortunately, the local we-have-it-all store was open until midnight. Not so fortunately, it was crowded with *other* parents whose children had *also* just presented them with the same list.

On the second day before Christmas, my father-in-law decided to string more lights outside, but slipped off the ladder and wrenched his ankle in the process. In the meantime, the boys showed signs of coming down with the same stomach virus their sister had had.

I settled my father-in-law in the living room on the couch with an ice pack on his ankle and gave both kids crackers and ginger ale along with their own buckets in case they couldn't make it to the bathroom on time.

The rest of the day was spent keeping my allegedly ill boys occupied so they wouldn't kill each other, replacing the ice pack on my father-in-law's ankle, doing endless loads of laundry, and pulling Bad Kitty out from under the Christmas tree on a regular basis.

Sometime around midnight, I realized that in all the commotion I had forgotten to defrost the ham for Christmas Day dinner.

On the last day before Christmas, the rain that had started early in the morning turned into hail and then sleet. The weather forecaster announced that the winter storm watch had officially become a winter storm warning, and we should be prepared for any and all of the above: blizzard conditions, snow accumulations topping a foot or more, and single-digit temperatures (not counting the wind chill factor, which put us somewhere in the Arctic category).

That was bad enough. What made it worse was that I had to make an unscheduled run to the grocery store, since Charley had dropped a full gallon of milk on the floor. The *last* gallon of milk in the frig.

I had had a second one, but my mother-in-law had poured it down the drain the night before, saying "I know the 'sell by' date was December 28th but it smelled funny to me and I didn't want the children to get ill."

On Christmas Day, I dragged myself out of my bed, exhausted after everything I had had to do the last few days. And it wasn't over, since my family would expect the traditional Christmas breakfast of French toast, cheese omelet, fresh-squeezed orange juice and baked apples with cinnamon. Followed just a few hours later by the traditional Christmas dinner of ham, sweet potatoes, homemade rolls, and pecan pie.

However, the ham hadn't fully defrosted, I had forgotten to buy sweet potatoes and all I could find at the grocer's the night before was a twelve-pack of brownies. As for homemade rolls, I decided that it was either sliced bread or nothing.

Hoping that everyone was still asleep so I could have at least an hour of peace and quiet, I shuffled into the kitchen to be greeted by my mother-in-law. *And* the welcome aroma of fresh-brewed coffee. Not only had she made a fresh pot and cleaned up the dishes from the night before, but she had also started the morning meal preparations.

She handed me my much-needed caffeine fix, explaining, "I wanted to help out. You've really had your hands full the last few days"—surprisingly without any snarky addendum.

Just as I was taking my first sip, my father-in-law yelled for me to come into the living room, where he proudly showed off a fully lit Christmas tree, declaring with satisfaction, "There. It's fixed. Now if you can keep that damn cat out of the tree, it should stay lit through New Year's!"

While I was admiring his prowess and patience, Sarah, Charley, and Jason rushed into the room, shoved me into the easy chair (spilling half my coffee in the process) and demanded that I immediately open the Christmas cards they had made in school.

Sarah's had a drawing of what was presumably the two of us on the front and "Merry Christmas to the best Mommy in the world!" painstakingly printed on the inside, while the ones from the boys featured snow scenes liberally decorated with glitter, most of which dislodged and floated into my coffee mug.

Just as I finished wiping my eyes, explaining to my kids that "Mommy is crying because your cards are so beautiful," my husband came into the room, gave me a kiss, and then handed me a gift bag.

I peeked inside and found a brand-new pair of slippers to replace the ones Bad Kitty had thrown up in, my *own* box of raspberry cream-filled dark chocolates, and a gift certificate for a full day of treatments at Peace and Tranquility Spa that included a mani-pedi, hot stone therapy, a seaweed wrap and a full body massage.

I looked around the room: at the now-lit tree topped with a single-winged but still beautiful angel, at my mother-in-law handing out presents to my barely restrained offspring while my father-in-law kept a stern eye on Bad Kitty who in turn was eyeing the ribbons, and at my husband, who was feeding Lily her annual holiday treats from her own Christmas stocking.

He smiled at me, and I smiled back.

I love the holidays.

Christmas Present

"And so, Carol, we thought it would be a nice touch if you could put together a little concert for our guests as part of our Christmas Eve party. Oh, nothing very long," Mary added hastily, as though she knew what I was thinking. "Just maybe a dozen seasonal melodies to generate the Christmas spirit. Or Hanukkah spirit. Or whatever other religious or ethnic celebration that occurs in December. Or in winter. I mean, I don't want to seem like I am not being culturally sensitive. Or ethnically sensitive. Or—"

And here she stopped, looking both flustered and slightly frightened, like a kid who had accidentally blurted out a dirty word when he meant to say a more approved one.

I almost felt sorry for Mary. I say "almost" because this was also typical of her. She was woefully inadequate at her job as the Recreation Administrator at Green Pines Retirement Villa. Actually, I couldn't imagine *any* job that Mary would be good at. Not only was she disorganized and had no concept of how to plan anything, Mary always managed to offend *someone* by trying to be non-offensive to *everyone*.

The simplest undertaking, like buying the right dessert for special events, seemed beyond her. When Cliff Walters turned ninety, Mary brought a chocolate cake trimmed with pink roses with "Happy Sweet 16" across the top, and last summer she arrived with sheet cake emblazoned with "Best Wishes for Your Retirement" for the annual Fourth of July picnic.

With Mary, the one thing you could count on was that whatever the task, she'd somehow get it completely wrong in her attempt to get it exactly right. So when I learned that she was in charge of this year's Christmas-slash-Hanukkah-slash-Kwanzaa-slash-Boxing Day (for our sole Canadian couple) festivities, I knew that it would not go well. Not that anyone asked me. After all, I was just a volunteer, doing my bit twice a week as part of my Women in Business group's community service obligation.

I would rather have filled bags at the food pantry or answered the phone at the village park's office than be at Green Pines. It wasn't that I didn't *like* old people. It was more like they were an ever-present reminder of what *I* would be in the not-too-distant future.

"So, will you do it? After all, you used to play at our church—not that playing our piano would be as nice as playing the organ—and you did it beautifully." But Mary stopped again, apparently recalling that the reason I no *longer* played at Archangel Gabriel's was that last summer when I broke my right wrist, they had asked the wife of the deacon to temporarily take my place.

And somehow, by the time my distal radius fracture had healed, the "temporarily" had turned into "permanently" and I was out of a job. A volunteer job, to be sure, and one that I wasn't all that crazy about since I had to get up at six a.m. every Sunday for the early morning service.

But still it was *my* job, and a welcome break from dealing with my responsibilities as office manager at Bill's Book Bin. *That* title sounded much grander than it was, since my "office" was a five-by-eight corner in the back room, and the only employees I had to "manage" were Bill's two teenage kids and Mr. Parker, an octogenarian who preferred to read rather than deal with customers.

As for wanting to be part of the holiday event planning, or for that matter, *anything* involving the season, the truth was that this year I wasn't exactly filled with the Christmas spirit. Unlike in the past, my son Jack and his family wouldn't be coming home to spend the holiday with me. Instead, they'd be going on a cruise with my ex and his wife Liz, who had moved to San Diego ostensibly for the climate, but I also suspected to be closer to Jack.

"Dad said it was Liz's idea—that she thought it would be a nice change for little Danny and Julie, and easier on me and Anita," Jack said when I called him on Thanksgiving. "All we have to do is drive to the port and then board the ship instead of packing up the kids and flying across the country to your house—not that we don't enjoy doing it and seeing you and all," he added quickly. "So, Mom, I was thinking maybe we'd come home for Easter instead, okay?" as though I had a choice in the matter.

I agreed, but clearly my son knew I wasn't all that thrilled, especially since this would be the first time since the divorce that I would be alone on Christmas. And now here was Mary, the queen of last-minute scheduling, asking me to put together a musical program that would cover every ethnic, religious, and cultural holiday in December and play the songs on an out-of-tune piano. *And* have it ready in less than three weeks, even though I had a full-time job.

"Oh, and can you make sure to choose songs that they can sing along to? And have handouts with the words? And—"

I put up my hand to stop her before she came up with any more suggestions or ideas or tasks. "Okay, I tell you what. I'll come up with the songs, but I can't promise that I'll cover all the nationalities or religions or whatever. Now what time is this party?"

"Right after supper—around seven. And Santa is coming, too!" as though I was a six-year-old who could be placated by the promise of Old St. Nick instead of a sixty-year-old who would be spending the holiday alone.

Christmas Eve—this was getting better and better. Not that I had anything to do that night anyway. I would have just gone to bed after watching a couple of those traditional sentimental holiday movies while downing a glass or two of wine. But now, thanks to Mary, I'd be here, playing Christmas-slash-Hanukkah-slash-Kwanzaa-slash-Boxing Day holiday songs—and *were* there Boxing Day songs? I wondered—and then have to drive back home in the cold and dark.

Ho. Ho. Ho.

"Fine, fine, but in that case, I'm going to have to leave now so I can start planning," and I handed the box of ornaments to her and pointed to the six-foot artificial tree in the corner of the lobby that I was supposed to be decorating. "You'll have to finish this."

And without giving Mary a chance to object, I grabbed my coat from the office and left the center, stepping out into an ugly combination of sleet, snow, and ice. With any luck, I'd fall and break my wrist again and get out of the whole affair.

But I made it home without any mishap and spent the next few hours digging through my collection of sheet music in search of songs that wouldn't put too much of a strain on the vocal abilities of the elderly audience. "Jingle Bells," of course, which would be a lively opener, then "O Holy Night"—a French carol that I hoped Lisette and Pierre Dubois would appreciate—followed by "Joy to the World," "Deck the Halls" and "The First Noel."

I'd tell Mary to pass out the cider and cookies when I started "Here We Come A-Wassailing"—appropriate timing even if no one there would know exactly what wassailing meant. While they munched, I'd move on to "Silent Night" and then that World War II sentimental favorite, "I'll be Home for Christmas," after which would come "God Rest You Merry, Gentlemen"—another old English song which might do for the Canadians—and "O Tannenbaum" for any Germans in the group.

Hmmm, just two more to go... I leafed through the book and settled on "Away in the Manger," closing with "We Wish You a Merry Christmas" that I thought would be an appropriate end to the festivities.

I stacked the sheet music on top of the piano, made myself a toasted cheese and tomato sandwich and spent the rest of the evening trying to avoid anything on television that would remind me of the upcoming holiday—hard to do since it seemed every channel was infected with Christmas mania.

The next afternoon, I cleared off the piano bench and started rehearsing. And by the time I finished for the day, satisfied that whatever mistakes I might make would probably be unnoticed by the crowd (especially if they forgot to put in their hearing aids), the sun had long since gone down.

I drew the living room curtains, noticing that all the houses on my street were gaily lit with holiday lights, and more than a few had Christmas trees in their front windows. All except mine, that is. It looked more like Scrooge's place: no colored lights, no decorations, not a wreath on the door nor a candle in the window. After Jack's call, I had decided against decorating, telling myself (admittedly with more than a touch of self-pity) there wasn't any point in dragging all that stuff out if no one would be there to see it except me. It would be just one more thing to clean up and put away in January. But right now, I wished I had set out something seasonal, even if it was just Jack's Christmas stocking hanging on the mantelpiece.

The next day I stopped by Green Pines after work to drop off the sheet music so Mary could make copies for the partygoers. But before I could leave the front office, she waylaid me and thrust a batch of envelopes in my now empty hands.

"The mail for Hallway B was supposed to be distributed but I have had so much to do I couldn't get to it. So could you do it for me, please?" I started to shake my head, but Mary went right on. "Oh, please, Carol! They get so excited when they get their cards that I hate to make them wait another day."

"Fine, fine," I said ungraciously, and after pulling on the Santa hat she gave me—"For that holiday touch!"—I headed down the hallway, sorting the envelopes by room number. While some residents would be getting more than others, at least it appeared that everyone—from Mrs. Abernathy in Room 101 to Mr. Jessup in Room 125—would get some mail. Everybody, that is, except for Mrs. Annabelle Edwards in Room 120.

She was the newest resident, having just arrived two weeks ago, and from what I understood, had been pretty much keeping to herself. She ate in her room, refused to participate in any of the social activities and while not actively rude, had made it clear that she wasn't interested in being part of the Green Pines family.

Fine with me, I thought as I passed her room, where the door was shut as usual. I wasn't exactly in a friendly mood myself. I dropped off Don and Carla's mail in Room 122, made it into Katie Jackson's room next door where I set two envelopes on her nightstand without waking her from her afternoon nap, before stopping in at the last room where I found its inhabitant engrossed in reading—this time *Murder on Maple Mount*.

"Do you know who did it yet?" I asked, but Mr. Jessup just waved his hand at me without looking up.

"Okay, okay," I said and put the envelopes on his side table. "I'm going now," getting a grunt in reply. I closed his door and then turned back toward the office. But as I approached Room 120, I was surprised to see that the door was open. And even more surprised to see the Edwards woman standing there, leaning heavily on her cane and apparently waiting for me.

"Damn," I said under my breath, and then gave her a smile. "Hello there," but she just looked at me.

"I don't suppose you have any mail for me." Her tone was definite, but I thought I detected a slight undercurrent of hope, so I tried my best to put a positive spin on my answer.

"Not this time but it takes a few days for forwarded mail to make it all the way to the new address," I said with a smile. "Maybe tomorrow or Wednesday," thinking to myself that by the time I came for my volunteer stint, the envelopes should have been distributed so I'd be able to avoid a repeat of this conversation.

Something in the look Mrs. Edwards gave me indicated that she knew not only knew what I was thinking, but also, she didn't really expect anything to come via the postal service. Against my better judgment, I moved a little closer.

"I'm not usually here on Mondays, but I stopped by to drop off the music for our upcoming holiday show. Did anyone tell you about it?" And when she shook her head, I went on. "It's taking place after dinner on Christmas Eve in the community room. There will be holiday cookies and songs— do you sing?" more to gauge how much attention she was paying to me than to get an answer. Even though the hallway was brightly lit, I couldn't really make out her expression since her room was dark and she was standing in the shadows.

"I used to," and to my surprise, Mrs. Edwards began to sing the opening to "O Holy Night" in a low voice. But then she stopped after the first few lines and turned, going back into her room and closing the door behind without another word.

"Okay, then," I said to myself, shaking my head as I went back to the office. Not that I necessarily wanted the conversation to continue, but the abruptness of her departure was unexpected.

"That's how she's been since she came here," Mary said when I mentioned it to her as I gave back the Santa hat. "She hardly talks to anyone, and she won't come to any of our get-togethers. I know it's hard to adjust but honestly, that Edwards woman doesn't even want to try!"

"Did you know she can sing?"

As soon as the words came out of my mouth, I wanted to call them back. I knew what would happen. Mary would see this as an opportunity for me to involve the old lady in the show—something I definitely didn't want to do. For one thing, I was trying to keep it as simple as possible. And for another, I just wasn't in the mood to try to make someone else happy when I was hardly full of joy myself.

But it was too late. Mary seized on them like a dog with a bone. "What a great idea, Carol!" she exclaimed, not that I recall expressing one. "You'll be back on Wednesday, right? Then the two of you can start rehearsing together! And since the show isn't for another two weeks, you'll both be ready to perform!"

"I'm not sure about this," I started. "Suppose she doesn't want to do it? And besides, I have things I have to do before the holiday," scrambling for some excuse. "You know, decorating and baking—"

But Mary interrupted me with a wave of her hand. "Oh, come on, Carol. Surely you can spare a few hours. And it just might be what's needed to make her feel more at home. Do your best to talk her into it! Consider it a Christmas present to her, something you're doing in the spirit of the season."

Uh, huh. What she didn't know was that my holiday mindset had evaporated when I learned I'd be spending it alone. But what could I say that wouldn't make *me* sound like some cranky old lady? Nothing. So, I simply nodded and left for home where I spent the next few hours wondering how I could get out of this latest challenge.

Not that I could count on Mary for any help. After dumping it on me, her contribution would be an endless series of questions about whether I had convinced that woman to do something that she most likely didn't want to do. And that was going to be even harder than I expected since, as usual, Mary had thrown a monkey wrench into the works. When I arrived at Green Pines Wednesday after five p.m., she was waiting for me in the office, the familiar flustered look on her face that boded no good.

"I stopped by Mrs. Edwards' room and just casually mentioned the holiday concert and said that it would be nice if she would consider singing a song or two, but she said no. Just flat out refused! So I thought maybe you could convince her," throwing a hopeful glance my way.

Why she thought that I don't know. I had certainly never demonstrated any skills when it came to persuading people to do what I wanted, and besides, my exposure to the Edwards woman was limited to that one encounter—hardly enough to establish any camaraderie. But since it would be faster to propose it to her and come back with the expected negative response than stand here and argue with Mary about my unsuitability for the task, I set off on what was most likely a doomed attempt.

The door to Room 120 was closed as usual, so I knocked lightly, hoping Mrs. Edwards wouldn't hear me. But then I caught what sounded like "Come in," and sighing, went inside. The room was dark, and I wondered why she didn't at least have on a lamp.

"Mrs. Edwards?" I called tentatively, still standing by the open door to take advantage of the light from the hall.

"Well, don't just stand there. Come in!"

I could barely make out her shape in the rocker, so I moved closer, catching my toe on the corner of the bed.

"Damn it!" I swore without thinking, and then added, "I'm sorry."

But she just said, "You *could* turn on the light, you know, especially if you're going to be banging around into everything."

As I came closer, she switched on the floor lamp next to the chair. "I suppose you're going to try to talk me into singing at the show."

It was a flat statement—hardly an encouraging beginning—but I took it anyway.

"Well, yes, I was," in a bright cheery tone that I *so* detested when people it used on me when they were trying to convince me to do something I didn't want to do. "When I heard you the other day, your voice was so lovely and I thought it would be a nice addition to the show and besides, it would be a way for people to get to know you—since you're new and all." I stopped there because I had run out of reasons.

"Humph."

Luckily any further negative response was interrupted by Julie, one of the aides, who was carrying a dinner tray. "Here you go, Ms. Edwards, your supper tray, just as you requested. Although," and she looked at it critically as she set it on the end table, "there really isn't much there. I mean, just your tea, a cup of soup and some crackers. You need to eat more."

"Thank you, but I'm not that hungry" was the only response Julie received. But she must have been used to it because, after shooting me a quick half-smile, she left the room.

"I hate being called 'Ms. Edwards.' My name is 'Mrs. Edwards.'"

It wasn't much to go on, but I took it as an indication that I could at least keep talking. "Well, Mrs. Edwards, I hoped you would reconsider about singing. And it wouldn't be for the entire show. Maybe just one or two songs. I can even give you the list and you can pick the ones you prefer."

No answer, and I wondered why I was trying so hard to get the old lady to participate. After all, it wasn't as though I had a vested interest in putting on this concert. Frankly, I'd rather not do it at all and instead spend my Christmas Eve at home. Alone. All by myself.

Stop it, I told that whiny voice in my head, and took a deep breath. "Well, anyway, if you change your mind—" and started toward the door.

"I didn't say I *wouldn't* do it," she said, and I stopped.

"But Mary told me—"

"Oh, that woman is a pain in my ass," her response startling me—not because I disagreed, but because I hadn't expected her to use that word. Mrs. Edwards just didn't seem the type.

"Quite frankly, she was so persistent that I thought the only way to shut her up was to say no. There aren't many things people my age get to refuse to do, you know. Someone is always telling us what to eat or drink, what medication to take or treatment to undergo. It just felt good to be able to tell someone I didn't *want* to have to do something. Even if I did," the last spoken so low I wasn't sure if I heard her correctly.

I wasn't sure what to say, although I could relate to the reason for her response and even applauded her for having more gumption, as my mother would call it, than I did when it came to Mary. Instead, I settled on the last part.

"So, you'd *like* to sing?" I asked tentatively.

"No, I like to *sing*," emphasizing the verb. "But I don't want to get up in front of a group of people I don't know and do it all by myself."

She paused for a moment and then continued, almost as though it was against her better judgment. "Every year, our church would have a holiday concert, and Charles and I would sing together. Charles was my husband," she added, glancing up at me. "He was a wonderful tenor and I'm a soprano, and when we sang together everyone said that we were the perfect match. And we were, in singing *and* in life. But then he died."

She stirred restlessly. "And I've no intention of singing alone. I never did it before and I'm not about to start now."

I didn't know what to say. Was that why she was at Green Pines instead of at her own home or living with a son or daughter? How long ago had he died?

"Last January," answering my last question even though I hadn't voiced it. "I woke up and he was gone, just like that. They said it was a heart attack."

There was nothing in her voice that indicated grief, but something in the way she shifted in her chair reminded me of the way you move when something hurts and you can't make it stop.

"I'm so sorry," but she waved my words away as though they were more annoyance than comfort.

"I came here because my daughter didn't want me living on my own. Catherine is a lieutenant colonel in the Army, and she's based overseas." She pointed to an eight-by-ten picture of a woman in an Army uniform on her nightstand. "I was hoping she might be able to come home for the holiday, but it doesn't seem likely, especially since she took an emergency leave when her father died."

She stirred her tea, releasing a slightly seaweed smell in the room. "This is Sencha tea. My daughter brought it when she came back from Japan for the funeral, and since then I order it online. Oh, not because I like it all that much," pausing to take a sip, "but because it makes me think of her and how we sat together for days with cups of tea while we dealt with the paperwork after her father died."

And there it was again: that movement that belied the calm, practical tone in her voice. I didn't know what to say or even if I should say anything. But she saved me from responding with some cliché that we both knew would be pointless.

"I'm sure you have something to do instead of being here. And besides, my soup is getting cold."

I took that to mean that it was time for me to leave but just as I opened the door, she spoke again. "When will you be rehearsing? I assume," she added, "you do intend to see if the piano is in tune before the event."

"I'll be back on Saturday after lunch," I answered, but when she didn't say anything further, I added, "Well, it was nice talking to you" and left the room.

For the rest of the week, I tried to push the conversation out of my mind—not that hard to do during the day since there were shipments of books that needed to be set out for holiday shoppers. But at night I could hear her voice in my mind, and behind it, sense her loneliness. After learning even just that little bit about her story, I was more than a little ashamed of my own attitude. Sure, it was disappointing that I wouldn't see my son and his family at Christmas, but they were still alive and there were future holidays to think about that we could enjoy together. But not for Mrs. Edwards. She'd never spend another holiday with her husband.

Well, there's nothing I can do about that, I thought to myself as I slogged through the snow on my way into Green Pines Saturday after lunch. As for convincing her to be in the show, I tried my best, although deep down inside I wondered just how much of an effort I *had* made.

I waved at Mary and then went on to the community room to see just how out of tune the piano was. Surprisingly, it wasn't nearly as awful as I had expected, although I'd still tell Mary to get it fixed before the show—not that I had that much hope for it to happen.

One by one, I worked my way through the songs, and even the occasional appearance of a staff member or resident didn't bother me. After all, I was used to playing in front of an entire congregation. So, I didn't even look up when the door opened yet again. But then, I sensed someone coming toward the front and I looked up to see Mrs. Edwards.

"Well, considering the condition of the equipment, it doesn't sound too bad," she said, which I took to be a compliment of sorts.

Of course, right then I hit the wrong key and flushed, like a child performing for a strict teacher who knew she had failed. But surprisingly, she didn't say anything, just came closer and lifted the stack of music from the bench next to me.

"These are songs you're going to play?" and I nodded. "You don't have my husband's favorite in the stack," and when I looked up at her she added, "'White Christmas.' We would sing it together at the close of the concert" and she began to sing the opening lyrics before stopping.

I smiled up at her. "You really do have a beautiful voice," and then worried that she thought I would pull a "Mary" and start hassling her to be part of the show. But she didn't answer.

"Well, I better keep practicing, then" and I started on the last song on my list: "We Wish You a Merry Christmas." I figured she would leave but instead she stood there, one hand leaning on her cane, the other still holding the sheet music I had already played. I finished the last few chords and then stood up.

"You're done?"

I nodded. "For today, at least. I need to do some grocery shopping and the weather report said to expect sleet, so I want to be home before it gets too bad."

I held out my hand for the pages she held, and she passed them over. Then, without even a goodbye, she turned and left the room. Well, so much for that, I thought to myself as I collected my coat from the office and told Mary to call the piano-tuner ASAP. I did my best and if she didn't want to participate, so be it. I was tired of trying to change her mind.

That's what I told myself anyway. But when she came into the room the following Wednesday just as I was doing another run-through on the now in-tune keys (in an unusual example of competence, Mary had managed to get someone to fix the piano), I was both surprised and pleased.

She handed me a few sheets and when I glanced at them, I saw it was the music for "White Christmas." "Now, I'm not asking you to add it to your list or that I would consider singing in the concert. I just thought that it would be nice to hear it all the way through."

I focused on the notes as Mrs. Edwards started singing. Then—"You hit the wrong key."

"Sorry. Shall I start again?" I looked up at her and realized that despite her sharp tone, she was struggling with painful emotion. *Of course,* and I could almost smack myself for being so unthinking. She was remembering her husband and all the times they had sung together.

"No. I'm going back to my room." She took the sheet music from me. "When will you be rehearsing again?"

"Probably Saturday," I said cautiously. "Even though I've been practicing on my own piano, I want to do another run-through on this one."

"Humph," and I couldn't tell if she thought my level of playing needed more than just a few practice sessions or if what I had demonstrated so far boded ill for the show.

"Would you like to come over—to my house, I mean—and accompany me while I practice?" God knows where that idea had come from or why I had proposed it. The last thing I needed was to bring some strange woman into my home to pick at my skill level until I had no confidence left. For a brief minute I was back at my piano teacher's house, where she would crack my knuckles with a ruler every time I made a mistake, while she barely acknowledged when I hit the correct keys.

I hoped she would say no. Instead, she nodded and said, "Fine. I'll be waiting in the lobby Saturday at one p.m. Please don't be late," and with that the old woman left the room.

I sat there and wondered what I had gotten myself into, and then why she even agreed to do that. Could it be that she was going to take part in the show next Thursday? And I was no closer to the answer when I arrived Saturday after lunch and saw through the glass door her upright figure, coat on and cane in her hand. I pulled up to the entrance, then got out to help her into the car, nervously checking for any bit of ice that could take her down and me with her.

And when we entered my house short time later, I was as nervous as a new bride inviting her mother-in-law into her home. What would she think of my housekeeping skills? I had cleaned the first-floor powder room, dusted the living room, paying special attention to the piano top and keys, and then, in a belated burst of holiday spirit, set out the foot-tall ceramic Christmas tree on the console table in front of the picture window. It wasn't much, but at least the tiny lights and star on top might set the right seasonal tone.

But I could have spared myself the worry. If she noticed the tree, she didn't count it worth mentioning. She simply stood there in the living room while I hung up our coats and waited for me to start playing. And for the next two hours, that's what I did. One after the other, I went through all twelve carols, and while she didn't accompany me on all of them, she did join in often enough to actually make it enjoyable.

But when we finished, I saw that her hand was gripping the head of her cane so tightly that her knuckles had whitened, and I hurriedly guided her to the nearby rocker. Stupid me. I was so intent on what I was doing that I had overlooked the strain it must be for her to stand there all that time.

"Would you like some coffee? Or tea? Although I don't have that Sencha tea you like. Or maybe some hot apple cider." I was babbling. I knew that but I was worried about her condition. For all I knew she was a diabetic and had missed her meds. Or a snack or something. What if she keeled over and died while I waited for the paramedics to arrive?

"I'm fine," and the look she gave me made me feel that not only did she *know* what I was thinking, she was amused by it. "But I wouldn't turn down a glass of whiskey. It's a little chilly in here, isn't it?"

I hurriedly flipped the switch to light the flames in the gas fireplace, and then rushed to the kitchen to get the bottle of Jack Daniels that was tucked in the pantry closet. My son had bought it last year as a Christmas present for me, although I rarely drank. But now seemed like a perfect time to start.

Twenty minutes later, we were sitting in companionable silence on the sofa, enjoying our small shot of liquor and the holiday cookies I had bought the other day.

"I love your voice," I said and then wondered if perhaps I should have kept my mouth shut. Would she take that as the start of another round of "Why won't you sing in the show?"

But she just nodded, finished her drink, and then said, "I'd like to go back now, if you don't mind. I want to take a little rest before dinner," and without waiting for an answer, she stood up and went toward the front door. She didn't say another word—not on the ride back to Green Pines nor when I helped her into the building. Once inside, she headed toward the hallway leading to her room, leaving me standing there, not sure of anything except that she was a law unto herself.

"Well, I gave it my best shot," I said aloud, once I was back home. I set the dishes and glasses in the sink, then took another cookie. "If she doesn't want to be in the show, that's her business, not mine!"

But when I returned on Wednesday for my final run through before the show, I found her waiting for me by the piano.

"Would you be willing to add one more song to the list?" and she handed me the music for "White Christmas."

"But—" I started to say but she held up her hand.

"That's the only one I'm willing to perform, so if you want me in the show, those are my terms."

Okay, then, I thought to myself. You're acting like you're doing me some big favor when all I am trying to do is be nice and get you into the holiday spirit.

I was considering telling her it was too late to make changes when she added, "Unless you've changed your mind" and I caught an undertone of something—uncertainty? loneliness?—in her voice.

"I'm sure I can do that," I said and saw her face relax a bit. "Do you want to run through it now?" and she nodded. But once we were finished, she left, and I rehearsed the rest of the songs one final time, wondering what had prompted her change of mind.

I was no closer to an answer the next evening as I watched the residents file into the room, some under their own steam, others using walkers or in wheelchairs. But whatever the differences in their physical state, they all displayed the same kind of excited Christmas Eve feeling like kids waiting for Santa. I watched for Mrs. Edwards, having saved a chair at the end of the front row close to the piano, but she wasn't with the rest of the group. Then Mary bounded to the front, her Christmas cap slightly askew, and clapped her hands to get everyone's attention.

"Happy holidays!" she called out and then waved toward me. "Tonight we're going to have a concert of favorite seasonal tunes, thanks to our lovely volunteer Carol, and we invite all of you to sing along!"

She grabbed the stack of stapled sheets that had the lyrics and proceeded to hand them out, while I started right in on "Jingle Bells" and tried not to let my disappointment over the absence of Mrs. Edwards affect me. It was just one more letdown this season, I thought as I launched into "O Holy Night." And once the show was over, the holiday would end with me going back to an empty house where there wasn't anyone there to wish *me* a "Merry Christmas."

Lost in my own admittedly self-pitying train of thought, I continued to play the next three songs almost automatically. I was just getting ready to launch into "Here We Come A-

Wassailing" when Mary came back up front and motioned for me to hold off.

"Now it's time for our own little elves to hand out refreshments," gesturing to the aides who were all gamely wearing Santa hats, "while Carol continues with the rest of the tunes."

While the cookies and punch were being distributed, I considered going to check on my soloist. But then Mary motioned to me to start playing again, and by the time I ended "God Rest You Merry, Gentlemen," nearly everyone was finished eating and ready to join in on "O Tannenbaum" and "Away in the Manger."

I had just about given up hope that Mrs. Edwards would appear when the door opened, and I saw her. She paused as though uncertain whether to come in, and then it hit me: this would be her first Christmas without her husband. Here I was, feeling sorry for myself because I'd be on my own this holiday, not even thinking about how hard it would be for her with her husband gone and her daughter stationed on the other side of the world.

I waved encouragingly to her, and after a minute, Mrs. Edwards made her way down front to stand next to me. I set the music to "White Christmas" in front of me and began to play. And she joined in, her voice as strong and true as though she was thirty years younger.

We were coming to the last few lines when the door opened again and standing there was a woman wearing an Army dress uniform. It was Catherine—I recognized her from the portrait in her mother's room—and I gave a quick look at Mrs. Edwards, but she was intent on following the lyrics on the paper.

Then, as her daughter came up to stand next to her mother, a rustle from the audience made Mrs. Edwards look up. Her voice faltered, then she continued, reaching out to grasp her daughter's hand as she sang the last few lines. Tears blurred my vision, and I almost couldn't see the keys. And suddenly, it didn't matter so much to me anymore that Jack wasn't there or that this wouldn't be like the holidays I had in the past. This was now, and in a way, the appearance of Catherine was a Christmas present to me as well, reminding me of all that I did still have: the love of my son and his family, even if it was sent long distance

I launched into "We Wish You a Merry Christmas" playing with all my might, and the whole room joined in, including Mrs. Edwards and her daughter. And just as I finished, I saw a text message appear on my phone: "Hi Mom! Merry Christmas! And start baking because once the ship docks, we're flying in to celebrate the New Year with you!"

Charley Catches the Christmas Spirit

To say that Charley lacked the Christmas spirit would be putting it mildly. It wasn't that he had a Scrooge-type personality or objected to the holiday on religious grounds or anything like that. He just didn't see the need to hang a wreath on the office door, put colored lights around the grimy window that barely let the sunshine into our space, or do anything else to mark the season.

"This is a business, kid," he would tell me when I would suggest each December first that maybe one small holiday ornament wouldn't hurt. "That's what I want this place to look like."

"Where's your Christmas spirit?" I'd ask, not really expecting an answer, before resignedly putting the decorations away.

But for a man so focused on having the office *look* like a place of business, he tended to take a more casual approach to the financial side, and it fell to me to start those uncomfortable conversations when the color in the checkbook's balance column shifted from black to red.

Today was one of those days, and it went the way all those talks tended to go. I gave him the stack of to-be-paid-or-else bills and he looked at them briefly before handing them back to me, saying only, "You worry too much, kid. Remember, it's all about the numbers."

That was Charley's stock phrase, the one he pulled out whenever I confronted him with some uncomfortable fact about the current state of the bank account belonging to Adams Investigation Service—Charley Adams, P.I.

I'd been working for him for close to ten years, and by now, I was able to predict the actions that would precede his statement. First, he'd look up at me as though I had no business being on *his* side of our minuscule office, disturbing him while he was engaged in something extremely critical like balancing playing cards one on top of the other or connecting endless miles of paperclips into a chain for no discernible reason other than to make me spend hours undoing them when I needed some to clip timesheets to invoices. Not that I needed all that many these days, given the current state of our client work, which was minimal, to put it kindly.

Then he'd sigh, an exhalation that came from the depths of his considerable bulk, and frown. Finally, he'd wave his hand as though my words—and possibly my presence, too—were just an irritating fly that could be swatted away.

But this time, it didn't work. This time it was serious. The information I brought to his attention this Friday afternoon, while uncomfortable and most assuredly unwelcome, needed immediate action that was far beyond my scope as receptionist/assistant/bookkeeper/general runner-of-errands.

If we didn't get some income, we'd be in the cold, dry darkness, due to the shut-off notices from the gas, electric and water companies. And *he'd* run the risk of operating without a license, since his renewal application was due right before December 25th.

"Well, the numbers don't look good, Charley," I said this time, not budging from where I stood. "If you don't do something and do it fast, I'll have to find another job."

This wasn't the first time I had threatened my boss with my absence, and while it generally worked (albeit only for a brief period of time), we both knew I wouldn't be submitting my resignation any time soon.

For one thing, the job suited me. If I wanted to take time off to get my hair cut, do some grocery shopping, or just lie around my apartment watching old black-and-white noir movies, all I had to do was forward the office phone to my cell—not that client calls were all that frequent—so as not to disturb whatever Charley was doing.

And for another, it wasn't as if I was the most employable person in the world. My rather checkered work history included brief stints as a cashier, inventory counter, customer service rep and telemarketer. This would have been acceptable if I were in my early twenties and fresh out of college, or in my late thirties and fresh out of full-time motherhood. But since I had neither a new degree nor offspring to blame it on, and was also well past the mid-forty mark, my résumé was hardly the type to impress potential future employers.

All of which meant that not only was Charley stuck with *me*, but I was also stuck with him—at least as long as the company stayed open. Which brought me back to the topic of today's conversation, one he was doing his best to pretend didn't exist as he continued the critical (at least from his perspective) task of balancing the loose change from the cash drawer into a pyramid.

But I could wait him out this time—not only because I had nothing better to do since my inbox was bare of anything that looked remotely like work, but because I knew it wouldn't be long before he ran out of quarters, dimes, and nickels. I had taken most of them the day before when I went to the dollar store to buy boring necessities like toilet paper and tissues.

Charley cleared his throat, and I knew that meant he had something to say that, at least in his mind, would be momentous. Or significant. Or at least shift the conversation in another direction.

"Ooookaaaayyy," he said finally, drawing out the syllables while he swept the coins into a very small pile. "So, McCallister, what would you suggest?"

His use of my full last name instead of my first (Terry) or more commonly "kid" (even though I was within a decade of his age) signaled that he was willing to take me seriously, which didn't bode well since it rarely happened. The last time was when he received a letter from the IRS that darned near put him in the cardiac ward and required a quick sale of what few assets he still owned to pay his tax bill.

I knew that calling me "McCallister" meant that, one, the situation *was* really dire, and two, he had already given it some thought.

"Well," I said cautiously, since I hadn't gotten much further in my own consideration of the problem than identifying it, "I suppose we could advertise. You know, in the paper or on social media or something." He looked at me pityingly as if I was a second-rate marketing student who would never earn her degree, and then smiled.

"Or I could go fishing where the money is and catch some likely prospects." He pushed a letter across the desk to me. I didn't recognize the name at the bottom—Adam Smith—so went straight to the contents: a brief request for Charley to present a one-hour seminar on the danger of identity theft at a holiday luncheon for the Carol County Business Association. The most important piece of information, at least from my perspective, was the honorarium: $200.

"And before you ask, yes, I called him and yes, I'll do it and yes, it's on the calendar." This was Charley's name for the bulletin board where he pinned scraps of paper noting dates, times, and locations of client appointments. "So, what I need *you* to do," swiveling away from me, "is to write it up. The presentation, I mean. And add in some useful statistics and warning signs."

"Okay, I guess I could," I said cautiously, feeling like there was still something he hadn't told me but unable to put my finger on it. "I can start Monday morning researching the topic and see what I can find. And then—" Before I could finish, he turned back to face me, his upraised hand stopping me in mid-sentence.

"The *luncheon* is Monday," pointing to the relevant section on the letter. "And don't forget the handouts—a hundred ought to be enough. It's a pretty big group, I hear. Like I told you, kid, it's all about the numbers. And in this case, the numbers mean there should be at least a few fish I can reel in. So instead of standing here yammering about how you're *going* to do it, don't you think you'd better get started?"

And then he smiled at me as though he had just given me some great big gift instead of hours of work that would probably take all weekend.

So much for my plans of watching *Roadhouse Nights*, *Payment Deferred* and *The Maltese Falcon* as well as *A Christmas Carol* and *The Bishop's Wife* (in deference to the upcoming holiday)— all courtesy of our library's stock of DVDs.

I sighed loudly enough to let him know what I thought of his idea and then said, "Fine. In that case I had better go to the library since our internet is shut off *again*," I emphasized the adverb, "and start researching, right?"

I didn't wait for his answer but went back to my desk, grabbed my coat, keys and purse, and left the office, closing the door with exaggerated firmness to further make my point. Actually, this worked out rather well, I decided on my way to my twenty-year-old rust bucket of a car that was covered with at least two inches of snow. I could stop at Bob's Wings and Fries and take advantage of the Happy Hour Special (a bucket of wings and two beers for $9.99) before waddling as fast as my sodium- and fat-indulgence of a meal would let me across the street to the library.

Once there, I'd pull up some stats, check out some books on ID theft, and then go back to my place. There, I'd either peruse the information and make copious notes (less likely) or dump them on the kitchen table before sitting in front of the television (more likely) until Sunday rolled around, and I really had to do something on the assignment.

Unfortunately, Charley must have suspected that my preferred plan was the second one, because he proceeded to call me. Repeatedly. Twice that night, eight times Saturday and then Sunday morning at six a.m. And each time he had the same question: "So, how's it coming, kid?" And each time I'd give him the same answer; "I'm working on it, Charley."

While I held off until close to noon on Sunday, the repeated intrusions ruined whatever enjoyment I would normally take from watching reruns. But I reminded myself each time I hung up the phone that if I did a good job, Charley might pick up some clients. And the income from those assignments would make its way into the bank account and ultimately to my paycheck.

So, despite having suffered from *weekend interruptus*, I was somewhat happy when I showed up bright and early Monday morning with a stack of handouts I had made at the copy place around the corner and his talk clearly printed in extra-large type. (Charley wouldn't wear his cheaters if his life depended on it.) Happy enough, anyway, to pay him a compliment on his attire: a suit jacket *and* a tie—two items I didn't even think he owned. Every other time I saw him, he would be in jeans and jersey emblazoned with a college logo from a high-priced school that I knew he hadn't attended.

"Looking good, Charley," I told him as I dumped the paperwork on his desk.

"Well, you're not," he answered, looking at me critically. "Don't you own anything nice?"

I glanced up at him in surprise, not because of what he asked but because he had never before remarked on my attire. I was wearing my usual Monday morning outfit: running pants and my "Coffee is my lifeblood" sweatshirt that a local café had given away to customers who filled up their frequent drinker card six months in a row—which explains why I had two more hanging in my closet.

"That's not the impression I want to make on this crowd," he continued. This from a man who only went to the barber when his comb-over refused to stay combed over.

"I'm coming, too?"

He nodded in the affirmative. "Of course," as though we had discussed it, which I knew darn well we had not. "So go home and change into something that looks businesslike."

When I frowned, he added persuasively, "Remember, it's a free meal. And if you play your cards right and somebody doesn't show up, you might even be able to sneak *their* meal into a doggy bag for later."

He had me there. I was never one to pass up a freebie, especially since my fridge was woefully short of anything that looked like consumables. A quick run home, an even faster search through my wardrobe, and I was back wearing what I considered professional attire: a pair of black pants and a black jersey. It would have to do since everything else either needed washing or mending—or both.

While I was gone, Charley apparently perused my report— if the highlighted sections were any indication. Fortunately, the man had a memory the size of his girth, and that coupled with his gregarious nature made him a hit at the presentation. I did my part throughout the talk, passing out the sheets on how to how to avoid identity theft and what to do if it happens, but it was Charley who was the big attraction, literally and figuratively.

Men liked Charley because he could talk about sports with the best of them, and women liked Charley because he flirted with them. And while the information I had researched was useful and well written (if I do say so myself), it was Charley's delivery that made the difference.

I wasn't surprised that the one hour turned into two, with Charley patiently answering questions while alternately handing out his business card and eating reindeer and Santa cutout cookies from the overstocked plate he stashed on the corner of the podium. But I *was* a little taken aback when, as the attendees finally started taking their leave, one diminutive white-haired lady that I judged to be well into her eighties remained at his elbow.

If she had the hots for Charley, she'd be cradle-robbing, I thought, smiling to myself as I came up to where they were standing. Then I heard the tail end of her words and my smile made it all the way to my face.

"So even though I hate to think that someone I trusted would use my credit cards without authorization, I have to face the facts. But before I go to the police, I want to be absolutely sure that she did it and understand *why* she did it," she said in a firm, business-like tone that belied her age. "And that is why I'd like to retain your services—assuming, of course, that your fee is reasonable."

Charley gave me a quick look over her head as though to say *I told you it would be worth it,* and then looked back down at his newest and, in truth, only client, and pursed his lips.

"Well, I usually charge a hundred dollars an hour," he said, and I darned near dropped the overfilled doggy bag I had cadged from the server since I knew that he had never charged anywhere near that amount. "But since you're part of the association, I'd be willing to drop it to seventy-five." And then he paused.

That was a trick he had taught me when I first started at the company: go high with the bid, then drop it a little, like you were doing them a special favor. Then wait. Usually they bit, and if they didn't, he always had some alternative deal to offer: a flat rate or a bonus service for free.

She frowned, looked around the room as though debating her decision, and then answered decisively, "Make it fifty with a cap at ten hours and it's a deal."

It appeared that Charley had met his match, at least in the bargaining ring, and I waited to hear his answer. Of course, he'd *have* to take it. He knew as well as I did that we needed the money. But it was *how* he would agree he was struggling with.

Never act like you're easy, he would tell me. *Make it seem like you're doing them a favor. Otherwise, you seem desperate.* This was humorous considering he would say it while opening up yet another envelope from yet another bill collector.

"You know what, Mrs. Robinson," pausing to peer at her nametag, "I like you. I like the way you get right to the point, and I like that you are willing to deal with bad situations rather than bury your head in the sand. And because I like you, I'll do it at fifty an hour *with* a two-hundred-dollar deposit. Then, after ten hours of work, we'll see where we stand."

He gestured for me to come closer. "My assistant, Ms. McCallister, will take down your information and send you a contract to sign. Then once the paperwork is out of the way, I'll set up a time to get all the details of your situation. Now if you'll excuse me, I need to talk with Mr. Smith."

I knew what he really needed was to grab his check before the guy disappeared. I watched as he lumbered away, making a quick detour back to the dessert table where he grabbed two sugar-encrusted snowmen and a brownie that magically disappeared into his suit pocket before heading to the man with his check. Turning back to Mrs. Robinson, I was disconcerted to find her sharp eyes fixed on me. I had the uncomfortable feeling that she knew the state of our bank account, the absence of any other paying clients, and everything else that pertained to our operation.

"He's not the best. I know that," she said, confirming my suspicions. "But this isn't a hard job and if I went to some of the other agencies in town, they'd charge a fortune for what he could do at a quarter of the price. And it shouldn't take long to get results. I know what was done. And I'm pretty sure I know who did it. I just need the background details. Then I can decide if I want to pursue legal action."

She paused for a moment and then continued. "You know, I never would have expected her to do this. I've known Maggie for about five years now, ever since I broke my hip and needed part-time help getting things done around the house. I hired her because I wanted someone older, who would be a little more understanding and patient. She's always been reliable, trustworthy, kind, and considerate. And I pay her well—" naming a weekly amount that was almost double my paycheck. "I just don't understand why she'd do this."

"Ready to go?" It was Charley, itching to get back to the office and divest himself of his suit jacket and tie. He gave me a glance that said *let's wrap this up.*

"Once we complete our investigation, I'm sure the reason for her alleged actions will be clear," I said reassuringly as I shook her hand. "I'll mail you the contract first thing tomorrow morning."

Then I followed Charley to the exit like a little tender following a big cruise liner. Once back at the office, I drew up the contract, gave it to Charley to sign and then spent what little was left of the afternoon alternately promising our creditors that payments were coming and wondering why the credit-card thief Maggie would have done what she did. Assuming she *did* do it, and this wasn't a case of our client using her card and then forgetting where and when she did it until the statement came. Not that it mattered *why* she did it, I suppose, although that seemed to be the most important part of the alleged crime to Mrs. Robinson.

Perhaps what Maggie bought with the card would provide an indication…I opened my notebook to make a list of questions I'd ask when we had our next meeting, *after* Charley deposited the advance and it cleared. You never know with people, he had told me more than once. Even the most honest of them can stick it to you when it comes time to pay the bill.

Not that Mrs. Robinson looked like a deadbeat client, I thought, but just to be sure, I did a quick search online to get some background on her. Widowed in her late thirties, she had taken over management of the apartment rental business her husband had started and grew it from just six units in a rundown building in an equally rundown neighborhood to three twenty-unit sites in upscale locations throughout the city. These were units that *I* could never afford and that undoubtedly brought her a pretty penny from her renters since none of them had any vacancies.

I was impressed with her success, especially given that, when she took over the company, her competition consisted of male CEOs who undoubtedly expected the little widow to sell that six-plex for a song. But they were wrong, and she kept going strong, still running Robinson Enterprises even at her age.

Once the signed contract was received and the check cleared, Charley and I went to Mrs. Robinson's house for our first official client visit. Charley knocked on the heavy oak front door, and then, while we stood there shivering in the cold December air, he gave me a few last-minute instructions. Not that I needed them, since it was the fourth time he had told me what I needed to ask, but it did make me wonder if he wasn't a little more worried about our money situation than he had let on. But before my mind wandered down *that* path, Mrs. Robinson opened the door.

"Maggie is cleaning upstairs, so we won't be disturbed," she said, leading us into a small sitting room. She handed me a folder labeled "Maggie Carlson." "Everything you need is in here."

And she was right. A quick glance at the papers inside showed them to be a summary of Maggie's employment: the date Mrs. Robinson had hired her, her home addresses and phone number, and the dates when she cleaned, along with copies of the last six statements for four different credit cards, the fraudulent charges highlighted in yellow.

It didn't take Sherlock Holmes to see the relationship between the credit card bills and the cleaning schedule. It was, as the famed detective would say, elementary: after each visit to the Robinson home, there would be a corresponding charge on one of the credit cards.

But what struck me as odd was the nature of the bills. I expected something self-indulgent: hair and nail appointments, for example, or purchases from high-end stores like Angela's Boutique. But instead, the charges were for places like U-Bag-It (a weekly stop, I noted) along with Bargain Basement or New Again Clothes. The first two were grocery stores that specialized in dinged and dented cans, perishables approaching their sell-by date and off-brand toilet paper that could pass for 60-grit sandpaper.

As for New Again Clothes, it was a consignment shop that sold clothes at a fraction of their original retail price, most of them in a condition that was barely above rag-basket level. (I knew that because the jeans and sweater I was wearing had come from there.) Other charges were equally surprising: purchases at a discount store for kids' shoes and a couple for the walk-in clinic on the worst side of town. What was the story behind them?

I didn't have time to think more about it, since, judging by the sound of footsteps overhead, it appeared that Maggie was coming closer to the staircase. I hurriedly pushed the papers into the folder and then waited to see how Mrs. Robinson was going to explain our presence.

But instead, she led us to the front door, before the cleaner-turned-alleged-credit-card-thief made her appearance, saying only, "Thank you both so much for coming here. Call me when you have something to report."

Apparently, our meeting was over.

"So, what's the next step?" I asked Charley once we were back at the office.

"Why don't *you* tell me what we should do?" a question that surprised me because Charley rarely asked my opinion on anything more than what brand of toilet paper to buy or when our landlord was most likely to show up demanding rent money so he could dodge him.

"Well," I answered cautiously, "I suppose I could do some kind of surveillance, maybe follow her when she leaves the old lady's place and see where she goes. And take some pictures if she does any shopping with a card. And then," warming to the challenge because it was certainly more fun than trying to balance the company checkbook, "put together a timeline showing what she did, where she did it and when the crime took place. And then schedule another meeting with the client and show her what we learned and see how she wants to proceed."

I looked at Charley the way a dog looks at his owner when he brings back the ball that was thrown, waiting for him to figuratively pat me on the head. But all I got in return was a sigh and a look that indicated he had expected more from me.

"Remember what our client said. It wasn't just confirmation of the *what* but also the *why*. That's the other answer she wants."

I hung my head. He was right. Judging from what Mrs. Robinson had said to both of us, she was bothered more by the betrayal of trust than she was by the sums that had been taken. That surprised me because, given her success in running her company, I had pegged her as a shrewd business owner, not one who allowed emotion to cloud her judgment.

As Charley had often said, sentimentality had no place in business. "If you're nice to people, then they will try to take advantage of you," he would tell me, and if at times he sounded more like a cheapskate than the guy who always gave me my birthday off with pay, I put it down to his nature, the economy, and the tough business we were in.

"So how do I do that?" I asked.

"That's up to you to figure it out. Actually," he swiveled his chair so he was looking out the window, "I was thinking this might be a good case for you to run point on."

Charley was just full of surprises today, I thought. He had never let me take the lead on anything bigger than dodging creditors or chasing down deadbeat clients. I looked at him, waiting for an explanation but clearly he wasn't going to give me one. I shrugged, mumbled something about how I appreciated his faith in me and went back to my desk.

While I waited for inspiration to strike regarding the reason for the cleaner's behavior, I started working on my list of when and where to do the surveillance. If I used the statements as a guide, I had a week before I had to show up at U-Bag-It, since, based on the credit card statements, she only went there every seven days.

"So that's how she did it," I said aloud. "She swaps out the cards on each visit, replacing one while she takes another. So even though she goes to the same places, it's not as obvious. But still, the old lady should have caught it sooner. Once or twice, maybe, but this often? How did she miss it when she paid the bills?"

"Because the payments were pulled automatically from her bank account."

I jumped. I hadn't heard Charley come over but there he was, leaning over my shoulder to look at my list.

"She has cataracts, so the statements are probably hard for her to read," he continued, and I looked at him in surprise. "I saw right away that her eyes looked a little cloudy. You know, if you want to be any kind of detective, you need to pay attention to all those details," obviously taking a certain amount of satisfaction at my lack of perception. "I figured she probably minimized the amount of reading she had to do. But something must have triggered her suspicions and then she started checking into to it."

I nodded slowly. That made sense. "So, if my list is right, then I should start the store surveillance next Tuesday since that's when she cleans Mrs. Robinson's place."

"And in the meantime?" prompted Charley.

"I guess I could check out where she lives," ridiculously pleased that I had come up with more ideas. "Do a drive-by to get a sense of how she spends her money and, well, everything," I added lamely but Charley just nodded and smiled like I was a puppy he was house-breaking who had managed not to pee inside.

"Good idea, and you should probably do that now." He handed me a ten-dollar bill. "Put some gas in your car so you don't run out," knowing my propensity for riding the big E. Sometimes I could go three days before the fuel indicator stopped flashing and stayed red.

I took the money even though I still had at least an eighth of a tank of fuel, and after noting down the Maggie's home address, fired up Bessie and hit the road, trying to ignore the sounds from underneath my car that indicated a muffler issue or possibly something worse.

"I'll get to it. I promise," I said, patting the dashboard. The car may be old, and it may be sporting more than a few dings, dents, and rusty areas, but I loved it. It was familiar and reassuring, like a pair of old flannel pajamas: despite being worn in places and with buttons just hanging on by a thread, it was still comfy and cozy.

Twenty minutes later, I was cruising past Maggie's home, where I was surprised to see a half-built snowman in the yard and two sleds propped up against the rusty wrought iron porch railings. I thought Mrs. Robinson had said Maggie was well into her fifties, but this looked more like a house where a young family lived.

I parked a little farther down the street and waited to see if Maggie showed up in her Ford Focus—a car that I had noted earlier sitting in our client's driveway that was similar in condition to my old beater. I was pretty darn sure it *didn't* belong to Mrs. Robinson.

It didn't take long before my patience was rewarded. First came Maggie's egg-yolk yellow vehicle pulling into the snow-covered drive, then right behind it a school bus, from which erupted three kids all screaming "Grandma! Grandma!" So that answered my question about the kid stuff. She was either babysitting or they stayed there. That added a new wrinkle, since nothing our client had said indicated that Maggie lived with family members.

"But she didn't say she didn't," I reminded myself, and then watched as the three kids piled into the small car before Maggie backed down the drive. Since I didn't know where they were headed, I decided to follow them as long as my fuel held out. Fortunately, the trip was a short one, ending in the U-Bag-It parking lot that conveniently (at least from my perspective) also had a gas station. I watched while Maggie and the kids went into the store, then, after putting as much gas in the tank as ten bucks could buy, followed them inside.

Even though I knew she hadn't seen me at the Robinson house, I still wanted to keep a low profile, so I grabbed a cart and proceeded to act like a normal customer—not hard since my cupboards were bare and I had planned to go shopping anyway. I even detoured down the holiday decor aisle, buying a new string of lights for my apartment and the biggest wreath I could find for the office door, as much to aggravate Charley as to establish some Christmas ambiance.

Ever since that first December after he hired me, when I put up a fake Christmas tree and he made me take it back down, growling that the holiday was just all about the money, we had engaged in an annual battle. I'd put up something seasonal and he'd take it right back down. It was a fight I was determined to win someday—hence my purchase of the wreath for this year, even though I knew full well he'd remove it as soon as my back was turned.

It wasn't until I hit the breakfast food aisle that I caught up with Maggie where she was holding a box of wholegrain cereal. I recognized that look on her face as her glance went from the box to her already loaded cart and back again, since it was the same one that was probably on mine as well. She was obviously calculating how much she had already spent and whether she could also buy that super-size box of bargain cereal.

I was confused. If she was using the old lady's card—assuming facts not in evidence, in courtroom terms—why would she worry about the total? And if she was using her own money, did that mean she had decided to mend her erring ways?

She turned her head in my direction, and I looked away, grabbing the first item I could find: Monster Munchies—a teeth-rotting combination of mini-marshmallows and sugared flakes.

"The kids love that one," and I turned to find her standing next to me, a smile on her face. "Every now and then I buy it for them as a treat, but not too often. The last thing I need are dental bills to fill the cavities they are bound to get!"

I smiled at her and set it back on the shelf, figuring this would be a good chance to try to pump her for info.

"You're right, and I don't need it either," making a mental note to buy it the next time I was in the store. "Is it hard to get them to eat healthy?" noting that her cart had carrots, celery and two heads of lettuce.

"Not really. They're good kids and my daughter," she looked away and swallowed hard, "raised them right. She was a nurse at the Lavender Rose Home."

I knew that place. It was where old people went when they couldn't live on their own and had no family to take them in. As for the past tense and the wave of sadness that passed over her face, I could only surmise that her daughter had died. Is that why she had the kids? No father in the picture to take them? I wasn't sure what to say next but luckily one of the kids—a girl who looked to be about nine—interrupted the conversation.

"Grandma, Jerry said he has to go potty," pulling at Maggie's arms. "He said he has to go *now!*" emphasizing the last word.

"Okay, Cara, I'm coming." Maggie shrugged and, giving me a rueful smile, set the box back among its brethren and then turned her cart to follow her granddaughter. It was clear that, unless I was going to follow them into the restroom, my chance for continuing the conversation was over for now.

Once she was out of sight, I finished my shopping, then hung around a bit. My idea was to get behind her in the checkout aisle and see how she paid for her purchases: with cash or with the credit card belonging to Mrs. Robinson? It was a good plan and it worked, especially because she was too busy corralling the three kids to pay attention to anyone behind her. Actually it turned out better than I had hoped, since when she pulled the card out of her pocket, it slipped from her gloved hand and landed on the floor. Quick as a shot, I grabbed it and handed it over, but not before I glimpsed our client's last name on the piece of plastic.

"Thanks," she said distractedly as she took it from my hand, not even looking up at me. She hurriedly slid the card through the machine, punched the button to skip the code, then grabbed her bags and the receipt, leaving the store with the kids trailing behind her.

So far, so good, I thought, as I paid for my few items and headed to my car. I had confirmed she had used Mrs. Robinson's card. Now to go back to the office, make some notes *and* hang the wreath. Then the following week, I'd tail her after she finished cleaning at our client's and try to "accidentally" run into her again.

And I did, this time at New Again Clothes. I had parked out of sight at our client's house and when she left right after lunch followed her at a safe distance. But instead of going home, she took a couple of left turns until she reached the consignment shop. I parked and then, while she was moving some boxes from her trunk into a cart, I slipped into the store, staying close enough to the entrance so I could keep an eye on her, but not so close that the clerks would watch me in case I looked like I was planning a grab-and-run.

Maggie pushed the loaded cart into the store and went over to the service counter, where she waited behind two other people. Then, when it was her turn, she opened the top box and started setting out stacks of women's winter clothes for the manager to look at them.

"They're all size six, freshly washed and with no holes, tears or stains," she recited. It was obvious that she had done this before.

I moved a little closer, my attention caught by the size she mentioned—not because they would fit me since *my* days of wearing single-digit clothing were far behind me, but because they obviously weren't Maggie's either. There was no way her plump frame would get into those items.

Did they belong to her daughter? If so, was she selling them *for* her? Not having the patience or the imagination to wonder any longer, I decided to barrel my way through it and pretend that it was the clothing that caught my eye.

"Wow, that's a really nice color!" randomly pulling an emerald green sweater from the stack.

"Please, ma'am, you'll have to wait your turn," said the store clerk, but I just ignored her and kept talking.

"I wish I wore that size!" and then turned to Maggie as if just noticing her. "Don't I know you from somewhere?" and frowned as though I was trying to place her.

"Yes, we met at the grocery store last week—the cereal aisle, remember?"

I let the clerk take the sweater from my hands, waited a beat, and then said, "That's right! You were there with your grandkids! They aren't with you today?"

"No, they're still in school. I don't like bringing them when I do this" and she tipped her head toward the stack of clothes. "It bothers them too much when they see me selling their mom's things, but…" and she stopped there and swallowed hard.

"I can give you twelve-fifty for all these," said the clerk and Maggie just nodded. She took the cash, shoved it into her pocket and then turned.

I decided to take a chance and touched her arm. "Look, I really don't need anything here. Want to grab a cup of coffee with me? I'm new in town and don't know that many people and I'm feeling a little lonely." I surprised myself not only at my imagination but also because it was partly true. I *had* been feeling a little lonely lately, maybe because of the season. It would be nice to sit with another woman and talk, even *if* that woman was a suspect. "My treat," I added, to sweeten the deal. Besides, I figured, I could turn the receipt in to Charley as a legitimate case-related expense.

Maggie took a quick look at her watch and nodded. "As long as it's somewhere close by. I need to be home by three— the school bus, you know."

"Joe's Diner has homemade apple pie today," volunteered the clerk. "It's two doors down and it's never busy at this time of day," she added helpfully.

For a fleeting moment, I wondered if she got a cut of the action for directing customers to the coffee shop. But then then the desire for a dish of cinnamon apple chunks wrapped in a warm flaky crust and topped with melting ice cream overcame me, and I smiled at Maggie. "Sounds good to me! Let's do it! I'm Terry, by the way."

Maggie smiled back. "And I'm Maggie. Maggie Carlson. It's nice to meet you, Terry. And a piece of pie sounds perfect!"

And that's how I found myself sitting in a small corner booth with our alleged credit card thief and chatting away like we were best friends. I started the conversation with a brief and not very creative lie about why I moved—divorce and the need to get away—and added that I was looking for a job.

"Well, I'm not sure this town has much to offer in that department," said Maggie as she smoothed her ice cream over the top of the pie slice. "I used to work at a grocery store but when the chains came in, all the independent places ended up closing and I found myself without employment. Since then, I've been getting by with part-time work with Home Angels. It's one of those home-care businesses with mostly elderly people as clients—you know, the ones who want to stay in their house but need help with different things like shopping or cleaning or trips to doctor appointments. The pay isn't all that great and there's no benefits, but it used to be enough until the kids came. Now it's getting harder to make ends meet."

"Your daughter…" letting the phrase hang out there to see what she would say.

"Car accident this past January. Caroline was coming home from work when a semi lost control on the highway and —" She stopped there, picked up her coffee cup but seemed to forget it was in her hand and just stared out the window.

"I'm so sorry." This was admittedly not much of a response but what else could I say?

She took a deep breath. "So, my grandkids came to live with me. They're good, most of the time anyway, and I like having the company. So, we're managing okay." I wasn't sure if she was saying that to me or to herself. "Speaking of which, I'd better get going. I have a couple other stops to make, and I promised Zack we could make brownies today. It's his twelfth birthday and he likes them better than a cake so that's what we'll have."

Maggie slid from the booth, and I followed suit, after first finishing the last bit of pie on my plate.

"Well, look, this was nice," I said awkwardly, not knowing how to end the conversation. Under normal circumstances, I might suggest another get together but I knew better than to start having a real personal engagement with someone who, if the old lady could be believed, was stealing from her.

"Me, too," said Maggie. "Maybe we'll run into each other again. Or if you give me your number, I can let you know if I hear of any job openings."

I paused for a moment and then thought, *What the hell. It's not like she could connect me with the business* and scribbled my cell number on a scrap of paper and handed it over. Then I picked up the check and moved toward the cashier, taking my time to pay the bill to make sure she was gone before driving back to the office to report to Charley.

"The thing is," I said after I finished going over everything I had learned, "she's a nice person and she's only doing it because she is strapped for cash because of the kids. If there was just a way we could present it to Mrs. Robinson so she wouldn't turn it over to the cops…"

I stopped there and waited, hoping Charley would come up with a solution to what even I recognized was an unresolvable situation. I knew Charley wasn't exactly a soft touch, but I figured even *he* would be moved by Maggie's plight. But that didn't seem to be the case. He just kept rearranging the paper on his desk without looking at me.

Finally, it came—that throat-clearing sound I dreaded. "Look, we were hired to find out if she did it and then present any other background information relevant to the case. And we did that. Now it's up to our client to decide whether she wants to turn this over to the cops. It's not our place to try to influence her decision."

He looked up at me when I stayed silent and then added, "If you'd rather not be part of that meeting, I can handle it. But this is part of the job. And it's not like this Maggie person didn't know that what she was doing was wrong. After all, she even took care to switch credit cards. That pretty much makes it an open-and-shut case."

"I know, I know," I said. "It's just…" and there my words trailed off. Good people sometimes did bad things. I knew that. But it all seemed so unfair. And if our client brought in the law, Maggie would most likely lose custody of the kids. There had to be a better solution, but I just couldn't come up with one.

"Okay, then. I'll set up a meeting for Monday morning and we'll wrap this up. Look on the bright side, kid," and here his voice did soften a bit. "This means I'll have the money to give you a decent holiday bonus. Won't *that* make you happy?"

"Yeah, yeah," I said with less enthusiasm than my voice would normally hold at the prospect of having a little more cash in my wallet.

"Okay. We're agreed. Now, *after* you take that wreath down," pointing to the office front door, "make these follow-up calls and set up some meetings for after Christmas." He handed me a list of notes: names from people who had attended the luncheon last month along with what they needed: a couple of spousal surveillance jobs and background checks on prospective employees. "But first write up your report on the Robinson case and get her invoice ready. Remember what I told you when you started. It's a business, kid. Don't get emotionally involved."

"Okay, okay, I know," I said, waving my hand at him. I detoured to the door where I unhooked the wreath and set it in the utility closet with the rest of the holiday stuff, then went to my desk to draft the results of the day's observation and then a summary about everything we had learned. And if I might have elaborated too much about Maggie's situation—her daughter's death and the struggle she was having paying her bills now that she had three more mouths to feed—I just put it down to wanting to give a full and complete report.

Then I spent the rest of the week setting up meetings with the new prospects and paying as many business bills as I could with what was in the business account. We were more flush than usual, thanks to the deposit from Mrs. Robinson, which brought me back to Maggie's situation. What would *I* do if I suddenly had to take on three kids on *my* skimpy salary? Would I steal from Charley? I'd like to think I wouldn't, but then people never know what they would do if they were caught between a rock and a hard place. And in Maggie's case, the rock was pretty damned big, and the hard place was one I couldn't even begin to imagine being faced with.

I was still thinking about it when my phone rang around seven Saturday night. I glanced at the caller ID, didn't recognize the number, and briefly considered letting it go to voice mail. But my curiosity won out and I answered the phone.

"Hi, Terry? This is Maggie, Maggie Carlson. You and I had pie together at Joe's Diner," she said. "Remember me?"

"Sure, I remember you," I said, surprised to get her call. "What's up?"

"Well, I wanted to let you know that there may be an opening at Home Angels—you know, that place where I work. I might be turning in my notice, so if you apply, you'll be on the list of people they'll call. It's not because I don't like the work," she added hastily. "But I heard that, come January, a factory over at Silver Springs will be hiring for the night shift and the pay would be a lot more than I make right now."

"Wow, well, that's good," I said. "But isn't that an hour away? And winter is a lousy time to be driving that far."

"Yes, I know," and I could hear the doubt in her voice. "But I don't have a choice—not really. I need the money. My landlord is raising the rent the first of the year, and I can't afford it on what I'm making at Home Angels. If I don't get a better paying job, the kids and I will have to move. As it is, I don't even have enough cash to buy them Christmas presents. And this year is going to be especially hard on them since it's the first one since their mother died."

She paused for a moment, as though debating whether she should go on, and then added, "And, well, the truth is I also owe someone some money and I want to pay it back."

I waited, but it seemed like that was all she was going to say about the debt. And although I didn't have any proof, I suspected she was talking about the money she stole from our client.

"Um, well, I guess you have to do what you have to do," I said finally. "But if you're working the night shift, who will watch the kids?" wondering if I was pushing it by asking about something that was not my business.

"I'll just have to leave them on their own. And after all, Zack is twelve and responsible for his age, and the two younger ones listen to him. I'll get Jerry ready for bed at eight and then leave for work, and with luck, I'll be back home before they get up for school. I'm sure they'll be fine. And it's only four nights a week."

But the more she talked, the more it sounded like she was trying to convince herself. I don't fancy myself as any kind of psychological expert, but even to my untrained ears, it was obvious that she didn't want to take the job because she worried about leaving the kids alone. Unfortunately, I didn't have any useful solutions to offer.

"Okay, but it doesn't seem like... I mean, maybe you ought to give it more thought before you decide," wondering why I was trying to talk her out of it and, for that matter, why I cared. After all, it wasn't like we were pals or anything. Whatever relationship we had developed was under false pretenses and now that the job was essentially over, we'd probably never see each other again.

"Oh, I have, believe me. But there aren't any decent jobs around here for someone my age that will pay enough to cover the rent increase. And well, kids grow, you know, and it's getting more expensive to feed them and get them clothes and everything. I don't know why I'm telling you all this, except that I don't have anyone else to talk to," she finished in a rush. "Anyway, I haven't quite made up my mind yet, but I wanted to let you know since you said you needed a job, and I think you'd do well at the agency. You seem like a nice person and all."

"Well, thanks. And I really appreciate the information," feeling more than a little twinge of guilt. Then in the background, I heard the kids calling her and her tiny sigh of exhaustion.

"Look, I have to go. The kids want their bedtime snack. Maybe we'll see each other at those exclusive stores we both shop in," she said with a short laugh that had an undercurrent of sadness in it.

"Yeah, maybe," I answered. "And listen, you and the kids have a nice holiday, okay?"

"Yes, and you too," she answered, and the call ended, leaving me to mull over the situation she was in and what, if anything, I could do about it.

For the rest of the weekend, my thoughts were on what Maggie was considering, with my fertile imagination coming up with scenarios that spoke to my fears. Something would happen to the kids while she was at work, or Maggie would have an accident on her way back from Silver Springs and never make it to the house. Or some well-meaning neighbor would find out the kids were alone at night and report her to the authorities.

And just the fact that I *knew* about it might make me complicit in whatever bad thing occurred. But what could *I* do?

I was still wrestling with the question Monday morning as Charley and I drove to our meeting with Mrs. Robinson.

"You're awfully quiet," Charley said finally as both we got out of the car and headed to the front door. "What's up?"

"Look, I know you told me it's a business and not to get involved, but…" and then I told him about the phone call and what Maggie was thinking of doing and how she wanted to pay back a debt that I was sure had to do with our client.

"And she doesn't even have the money to give the kids any gifts this year," I added. "It's the first Christmas since their mom died but when they wake up there'll be nothing there for them that might brighten up their day a bit!"

But when I finished, Charley just shook his head. "Look, kid, I agree that it's a tough situation she's in, and I understand that it's bothering you a lot, but it's not up to us. Whatever happens next is between our client and her employee."

He took the folder with Mrs. Robinson's invoice and the details of Maggie's wrongdoing from me before knocking on the door, adding, "All we can do is present the facts, okay? So let's get it over with."

But I noticed his voice held none of the usual enthusiasm in anticipation of receiving payment for the successful closure of a case. I knew he was right, but that didn't make me feel any better. And once we were in the house and Charley began detailing the damning facts that made it clear what Maggie had done, it didn't take much imagination to think about what could happen next if our client opted to bring in law enforcement to deal with the situation. The police and social services would be waiting at Maggie's house to haul her off to jail. The kids would be in tears as they were taken away from the only family they had left. And if there was a trial, I might even be called as a witness and have to face Maggie in a courtroom. I was so lost in that picture and the guilt I felt that it took me a few minutes to realize that Charley had stopped talking and was watching me.

"I'm sorry—what?" I said and looked at the two of them. I couldn't tell from the lack of expression on the old lady's face what she was thinking, but when I glanced at Charley, I could have sworn his eyes held a bit of encouragement.

"I said you had some additional information to share with Mrs. Robinson that might shed some light on Maggie's behavior. After all," he turned to our client, "when we first talked, you *did* say you wanted to know not just what she did, but why. And I think my assistant can give you some insights."

There it was. It was up to me to put Maggie's behavior in the best possible light: not to excuse her but to provide the motivation for her actions. Not that I expected it to matter to our client. After all, she *was* a successful business person, and I was pretty sure she didn't get that way by letting people take advantage of her.

All I could do was my best, I thought, and taking a deep breath, I filled in Maggie's backstory: her daughter's death that led to the grandkids moving in with her and the rising cost of feeding and clothing three growing kids, not to mention the upcoming rent increase. Then, figuring at this point I might as well tell it all, I even brought up her plan to work nights to make more money so they wouldn't have to move.

"And," I added, "she also said she had a debt to repay, which I took to mean what she owed you for the credit card charges. Not that she said anything about it to *me*, but I could tell it bothered her. The fact is, she *is* a good person—you said yourself that she seemed kind and considerate—and the only money she took was for her grandkids. And it wasn't a lot of money either, so maybe if you give her a chance, let her explain…"

My voice dwindled off as I looked at our client, hoping for some indication of sympathy or understanding on her face. But she just sat there, not saying a word.

After a few minutes of silence, Charley began to speak, his voice holding a persuasive tone that he rarely used on me. "You know, Mrs. Robinson, perhaps it might be possible to evaluate her actions in light of the bigger picture," he started. "I'm not excusing her behavior or in any way justifying it, but it's clear from what my assistant discovered that this was not done with malicious intent, but out of desperation. To involve the police would only make a bad situation worse."

He paused there, obviously waiting to see what impact his words might be having. For my part, I just sat there in surprise since Charley was the *last* person I would have expected to take the side of the wrongdoer. Maybe, I thought, it was my recitation of Maggie's financial problems that had moved him.

Finally, Mrs. Robinson began to speak. "Well, you seem to have done a thorough job. I assume that's the report you put together for me?" glancing at the file folder Charley held. "If you give me your invoice, I'll write the check now."

He handed it over to her. "The bill is inside, but there's no rush. You can drop it in the mail at your convenience." This was a surprising statement since I knew he preferred to get the money when it was offered rather than trust the mail *or* our clients.

She nodded, opened the folder, and took a quick look at the notes. "I'll take what both of you said into consideration." Then she stood up, adding. "Thank you for your time and attention to this matter."

Clearly, the meeting was over, and if I hazarded a guess, I would say that neither Charley nor I had said enough to sway her toward forgiveness. I looked over at Charley, but he just shrugged his shoulders and then we both got to our feet and followed her to the door.

I had done my best to explain Maggie's situation and now there was nothing left to do, I thought once we were both back in the car. I didn't have enough money in my bank account to loan Maggie, even if I could come up with a way to explain how I knew what she had done.

"Maybe she'll go easy on her," I said, as we drove back to the office. "I mean, it's not like Maggie didn't have a good reason for what she did." I looked at Charley but the expression on his face was hard to read. "And why didn't you take her money when she offered it? It's not like *we* don't need it!"

"Yeah, yeah, I know," he answered. "Look, let's call it a day. I'll drop you off at the office so you can get your car and then I have some stuff to do. I'll see you tomorrow, okay?"

"Sure," I said in surprise. It wasn't like Charley to give me half a day off with pay out of the blue, but I wasn't about to look a gift horse in the mouth. Besides, I was feeling more than a little down after the meeting and hoped there'd be something on TV that I could watch to take my mind off what would undoubtedly happen tomorrow when Maggie went to work and the old lady dropped the bomb about the credit card charges.

But I didn't feel much better the next day, even though I had binge-watched a series of movies from the forties while I polished off a twelve-inch pizza. I came into the office, depressed, and bloated, and even the sight of a stack of boxes in holiday wrapping paper piled on my desk didn't improve my mood.

"What's this?"

"Here," said Charley, handing me a super-size trash bag. "Put them in this and drop them off on Maggie's porch while she's gone."

"But—" I stopped talking when he raised his hand.

"It's just some stuff for the kids—for Christmas, you know. No matter what happens, they at least should have something under their tree."

It was the last thing that I expected to hear from Mr. "Remember it's a business" Adams. Maybe he *had* caught the Christmas spirit. If so, it was the first time in our acquaintance that it had happened. But I certainly wasn't going to point this out. Instead, I did as I was told. I had just finished loading the gifts into the bag when the office door opened and Mrs. Robinson walked in.

She headed right to Charley's desk and handed him an envelope. "I was coming to town so I thought I'd stop by and bring you your check," she said. Then she walked over to the window. "Did I ever tell you how I got into the landlord business?" Without waiting for an answer, she went on. "My husband Alan was the maintenance supervisor for Bexter Tool & Die for ten years. Then the company shut down, along with many of the other big employers around here. We had two choices: move somewhere else where he could find work or come up with a new plan. That's when he bought the first six-plex over on South Cabot and named it SC Place."

She paused, still looking out at something—the past, maybe? Then she shook herself slightly and went on, her voice softening.

"Little by little, Alan bought a few more places—ones in the better part of town—but he kept the Cabot one, even though it was costing us money to maintain. You see, the people who lived there were down on their luck. Some had lost their jobs like Alan had. Others were single parents trying to raise their kids or old people with no family to take them in. And all of them were just one life crisis away from ending up in that terrible county-owned housing project. Alan fixed up the place and even put in a play area for the kids, but he never raised the rent. He said the tenants were good people, and this was his way of helping. And it all worked out because the other places we owned were making enough of a profit to cover any shortages at SC Place. Then he died—he was just forty-two—and it was up to me to run the business."

Charley stirred in his chair, and I looked over at him, expecting to see his "Can you get to the point because time is money" expression. But I was wrong. He was just getting more comfortable, with a look on his face like a kid listening to a bedtime story.

"After he died, my accountant wanted me to sell the South Cabot place. He said it was more like Santa Claus Place because at the rent I was charging, it was a gift to people living there, and it was costing me money every month that I held onto it. But I told him I was keeping it. Maybe it wasn't financially profitable but there's more to life than money, you know. My renters were great people who needed some help and a decent place to stay, and as long as I could manage it, that's what I'd give them. Besides," and she looked over at us with a twinkle in her eye, "the rent from the other places I owned brought in plenty—more than enough to cover South Cabot and keep my income tax down."

She stopped speaking and came over to us, and something in her facial expression indicated to me that her little trip down memory lane was over. "Well, enough about that," her voice was back to the brisk, all-business one I was familiar with. "Now I want to talk to you about another matter. From time to time, my company needs the services of a private investigator. You handled this case quite well. To be honest," she glanced over at me, and I could have sworn she was trying to keep from smiling, "you did better than I expected. So, if you're interested, I'd like to put you on a monthly retainer—say $750 a month."

I looked at Charley in surprise. And when our eyes met, I could tell that her offer was the last thing he had expected as well. But I'll give him credit. Even though a retainer of that amount would almost meet our expenses, he didn't jump at it but took a few beats before answering.

"Well, I appreciate the offer," he said finally. "I think we can manage that—with the stipulation that it doesn't exceed fifteen hours a month. Any excess would be charged at my regular hourly rate."

"Or you can track your time and any overage would be applied to the next month's hourly budget," she replied.

It was like watching a slow-motion tennis game: she lobbed the ball at him, he hit it in return and then she batted it back to his side of the court. I just wasn't sure who would win the match.

"That will work," Charley said finally, as though he was doing her a big favor.

I released the breath I had been holding and mentally started calculating how I would spread out that monthly check to keep most of our creditors at bay. It looked like Santa had started his delivery before December twenty-fifth, and Adams Investigation Service was at the top of his list.

"Fine," said Mrs. Robinson. "Draw up the contract and send it to me and I'll sign and return it with a check for January. And have a nice holiday—both of you!" and with that, she was gone, like Ol' St. Nick who had dumped off a few unexpected gifts before heading back to the North Pole.

The door had barely closed behind her when I ran over to Charley. "Do you believe that? I never expected her to put you on a retainer!" And then, realizing belatedly that he might take that as an insult, I added, "I mean, of course you're worth every penny, but it just wasn't what I thought would happen!"

"See, it's like I told you—everything works out in the end," he answered. "Now don't you have something you need to do?"

He meant the gifts, of course—another unexpected deviation from the norm. Typically, it was all I could do to get him to donate to our building manager's annual holiday drive to support the local food bank. It's not that Charley was exactly stingy, but I wouldn't list generosity among his top qualities.

"Okay, okay, I'm going. But at least admit that you're happy about the money," since he didn't seem as pleased as I thought he'd be.

"I am, it's just…" and his voice trailed off as he looked at the bag of presents. "Well, I'd like to know what she decided to do about the Maggie situation."

Another surprise. Could it be that he was more touched by Maggie's plight than I realized? Certainly the gifts indicated that. Maybe there was hope for him yet.

"Yeah, me, too, but at least this stuff will help brighten the holidays a bit, no matter what," I answered. But I was worried as well. An early arrival from the man in the red suit would hardly offset the appearance of cops at her door with an arrest warrant for credit card theft.

Well, there was nothing I could do about that, I told myself as I grabbed the bag and my keys. I piled the bag into the car and then decided to make two stops before I went to Maggie's: one to Harry's Hamburger Heaven for a gift certificate to add to the gift bag and the second to U-Bag-It for a carton of Monster Munchies for the kids to enjoy Christmas morning. I reasoned that I had enough time since she wouldn't be done cleaning at Mrs. Robinson's for at least another hour.

But when I pulled onto her street, I saw that her car was still in her driveway. *Now* what was I supposed to do? And why was she there anyway? She should have been cleaning at our client's house. Had she been fired? And if so, did I bear some responsibility for that outcome, even though I was just doing my job?

I debated for a minute, and then, after parking in front of the house next door, grabbed the bag, ran to her house, and dumped it on her porch and then dashed back to my car, hoping to get away before she spotted me. But I was just two blocks away when my phone rang. It was Maggie. Had she seen me after all?

"Hello?" I answered after hesitating a minute, my brain scrambling for some explanation of why I had been at her house, especially since, as far as *she* knew, I had no idea where she lived. But I needn't have worried.

"I just got some great news and I wanted to tell you!" she said in a voice I hardly recognized: excited and relieved and happy all wrapped up in one. "Can you meet at Joe's Diner so we can celebrate?"

And even though I had planned to steer clear of any future meetings, my curiosity got the better of me. I answered, "Sure," and in less than twenty minutes, the two of us were seated in a booth, with our two donuts and super-sized mugs of coffee.

"What's up?" I asked and she gave me a smile that lit up the place.

"Last night I got a call from Mrs. Robinson—she's one of the clients I clean for—and she asked me to come over with the kids. She said there was something she wanted to discuss with me."

She stopped there and looked away for a minute, as though trying to decide how much to tell me, then took a deep breath and went on.

"Remember that money I told you I owed somebody? It was her—Mrs. Robinson. The truth is, for the past few months I had been using her credit card without her knowing about it, just to buy what I absolutely needed for the kids," she added hastily. "And I was going to pay her back, every cent and then some, when I took the new job. But when I went there—luckily the kids were on their best behavior—she told me she found out what I had been doing and that she wanted to discuss it with me."

She took a gulp of her coffee and then looked at me. "I was scared. I thought for sure she was going to call the cops. But she said everyone makes mistakes and if she had known about my daughter and the kids and everything, she would have helped me out. And she said that she believed I was a good person, and I must have been desperate to do something so risky. Anyway, she told me she had been looking for someone to manage a place that she owned and wanted to know if I'd be interested. And the best part is that it comes with an apartment!"

I damn near choked on my coffee. Did this mean Mrs. Robinson *wasn't* going to call the cops? "That's great news," I said. "Where is it?"

"It's called SC Place over on South Cabot. And the kids won't even have to change schools! Anyway, she said she'll take twenty-five percent out of my pay until the debt is cleared, and then everything will be fine. I mean, I still can't believe it!"

Maggie looked like someone who had just found out that Santa was real and he had given her everything her heart desired.

"That's fantastic!" I said, wondering why our client hadn't mentioned it when she came to the office earlier. "I'm so happy for you!"

"And then, when I left the house to meet you, I found a big bag of presents someone had left on our porch out of the blue! I can't believe it! Who would have done such a wonderful thing?"

Who indeed, I thought, but just smiled and then, after taking the last bite of my donut, I glanced at my watch as though I had to be on my way somewhere. "I have to go, but I am so happy for you and how things are turning out. And I hope you and the kids have a great Christmas!"

"You, too," she said, reaching across the table to grasp my hand. "And thanks for listening to me and not judging me about, well, what I did."

"Hey, we all do things that maybe we shouldn't, but seem like the only choice at that time," I said awkwardly. "And I'm so glad it all worked out. I really am." With a final wave, I left the diner, anxious to tell Charley what happened.

But when I got to the office, the first thing I noticed was that the Christmas wreath was back up on the door. *What's up with that?* I wondered, as I turned the knob.

Once inside, the smell of fresh-cut pine hit me and I saw the cause of the seasonal fragrance: a three-foot evergreen standing smack in front of the freshly cleaned window and tricked out with what looked like hundreds of ornaments and miles of twinkling lights. I closed my eyes then opened them again, certain I must be hallucinating. But no, there it was in all its holiday glory. And standing next to it was a beaming Charley.

"Holy cow!" I said, coming closer so I could get a better look.

"Well, what do you think?" he asked, as though having a decorated Christmas tree in the place was an annual occurrence, although we both knew perfectly well that it wasn't.

"Um, it's gorgeous," I said cautiously, wondering if Charley had imbibed some alcoholic seasonal cheer or if he had suffered a split-personality disorder. "I mean, it's the last thing I expected to see, but it looks great! I was just surprised, that's all."

"Well, I don't know why. I mean, it *is* the right time for it," as though *I* was the crazy one and he was just doing what he always did.

I let it drop and then reached out to straighten one of the ornaments that looked ready to fall. "No, no, you're right," I agreed. "And you really did a heckuva job on it. Maybe too great," I couldn't resist adding, noticing that one of the branches that had started to droop under the weight of three glass balls and two strings of lights. "There's a lot of stuff on this tree. Don't you think you may have overdone it a bit—maybe put on too much?"

Charley gave me a familiar look—the same one he always gave me that indicated he had expected more from me. Then he set the glittery star right at the very top of the tree.

"Nah, when it comes to putting ornaments on a tree, it's all about the numbers. What's wrong with you, kid? Where's your Christmas spirit?"

Holiday Reunion

"Who the—?"

The sound that had penetrated my sleep-numbed brain was my doorbell, unaccountably ringing at seven a.m. It was too early for door-to-door salespeople, and too late for nocturnal thieves casing the joint. That left only one category—yet another one of my relatives.

"Anyone would think I posted a 'Welcome' sign out front," I muttered as I slid out from under the bedcovers, then pulled the blanket back over Baby Freddie—not that he was a baby anymore, mind you. He'd be the first to tell you "I no *baby*! I'm *fwee*!" if you dared call him "baby" to his face. But that was the only way to distinguish him in conversation and in mind from his father Freddie who was chronologically three decades his senior but his equal in maturity.

"There's nothing wrong with Freddie that a good swift kick wouldn't solve," my father once said, and I had to agree with him. Just yesterday Freddie was eating peanut butter right out of the jar. Not the store brand either, mind you, but the organic one that cost me four dollars a bottle—an early Christmas gift from me to me. That was bad enough, but he had opted to skip the utensil route and was instead dipping his finger into the spread.

"For God's sake, Freddie!" I said, but he just lifted his eyebrows at me before screwing on the lid and putting the jar back where he got it.

Remembering the episode, I could feel my blood pressure start to rise. Before this, stress had never been a problem for me, but then I had never had a houseful of relatives descend on me like a horde of locusts, eating and drinking everything in sight—including, it appeared when I checked the refrigerator last night, my flavored coffee creamer. It was my one indulgence, and now it was gone. Oh, the *container* was still there—someone had thoughtfully set it back in the refrigerator—but the contents had vanished.

"Freddie again," I had sighed, pulling out a half-empty carton of skim milk. Maybe if I added a little vanilla flavoring, I could pretend it was the good stuff.

Pretending—now that was what had gotten me in this mess in the first place. My father had always warned me about my tendency to pretend, to be less than honest—in short, to be the polite little girl my maternal parent had raised.

"You're just like your mother, you know," he had told me time and time again. "If she was being held up, she'd apologize to the robber for not having enough money. You need to speak your mind, Cassie, or the world will walk all over you!"

Or in this case, walk *in* on me with luggage in hand: unannounced, unwanted, and clearly unmoving, at least for the next few days.

Aunt Mae was the first. She had interrupted the start of my cherished holiday routine: a pot of fresh-brewed coffee instead of the fast-food mud I usually gulped down on my way to work, and a bagel from Mrs. Schatskie's Deli topped with a generous load of cream cheese and strawberry jam.

It was Friday and the first day of my long-awaited Christmas break from my school cafeteria job, and I was more than a little irritated by the unexpected intrusion. When I answered the doorbell, I expected to find some kid selling holiday ornaments or magazine subscriptions, but instead discovered Aunt Mae, a suitcase at her feet and a smile on her face as though certain of her welcome.

"Why, hello, my dear. I *knew* you wouldn't mind."

Mind? Mind *what*? I thought, but before I could ask, she went on.

"Cousin Roberta's wedding is next Wednesday, and you *know* how expensive hotels are, and you *did* say I should come and stay at your place the next time I was in town."

Thinking back, I was sure I had never voiced those exact sentiments. Oh, I might have said something like Aunt Mae should come see me whenever she was in West Oakland. That would only have been polite and certainly safe as well since Aunt Mae rarely traveled farther than her own doorstep let alone all the way to my place, which was a good two hundred-plus miles away. And since Aunt Mae didn't drive and Uncle Carl never, to my knowledge, took time off from truck-driving for family events such as births, weddings and funerals, a Greyhound bus ride would have been my aunt's only mode of transportation.

"Cassie? It's okay, isn't it?" and Aunt Mae's expression clouded over. "I mean, I know I should have called, but your mother *said* you were going to the wedding and so I thought it would be all right…"

Her voice trailed off and I realized that I was still standing at the door, holding my bagel and my now cooling coffee in my hands while Aunt Mae's face started to pucker up like a kid who just found out that the Santa isn't coming after all.

"Of course it's all right," I said, with only the least tinge of resignation in my voice. "Remember your manners," I could hear my mother say—my mother, who was now enjoying a holiday cruise to The Bahamas with my father while simultaneously avoiding Roberta's wedding.

Setting down my breakfast, I picked up her surprisingly heavy suitcase—just how long *was* she planning on staying?— and led the way to my spare bedroom. Barely large enough for the double bed and dresser I had appropriated from my parents' house when they decided to move to Florida, it was the one place I could put a guest (or so I thought at the time). The only other bedroom (besides mine, of course) was currently doing double-duty as a home office *and* storage area, thanks to the autumn rains that had flooded my basement.

"I'll get some extra hangers," I said, and backtracking to my bedroom, I emptied a few of mine and brought them to Aunt Mae. Then I left her to hang her clothes in the tiny closet while I went to the kitchen to dump out my now cold coffee and pour another from the pot.

It would be fine, I told myself. It was just one person for just a few days. How bad could it be?

Twenty minutes later, while Aunt Mae was still unpacking her endless supply of lotions and face creams, the phone rang. It was the aforementioned Freddie, Aunt Mae's son, asking for directions to the house. Aunt Mae, it seemed, had forgotten something, and it wasn't an item of clothing but an item of information: to wit, that my cousin was *also* invited to the wedding and by extension to my humble abode.

"Ma said you had a nice place, and she didn't think you'd mind," he shouted, his voice drowned out by the sound of traffic. Freddie, it seemed, was calling from the road, so sure of his welcome that he set out without bothering to check with me first. If he hadn't forgotten my address, I would never have received advance notice of his arrival. Not that I could have escaped. Aunt Mae's presence precluded that possibility.

"When are you coming?" I asked, but the squeal of brakes drowned out all but the words "later" and "Gotta go!" before Freddie disconnected the call. This left me wondering *when* exactly he would show up, *where* I would put him when he *did* arrive, and *if* he would still behave as though his mere presence should be cause for rejoicing.

"How nice!" exclaimed Aunt Mae when I apprised her of her son's call. "You two never get a chance to visit! And you're cousins, after all. You need to keep in touch! Now what shall we have for dinner?"

Dinner? It was barely nine-thirty in the morning! But I was soon to learn that, for Aunt Mae, it was never too early to think about supper. I thought of my limited selection of foodstuffs, more suitable for my admittedly eccentric tastes (I have a regrettable fondness for macaroni and cheese laced with chopped pickles, raw onions, and canned salmon) than for that of my senior citizen aunt.

"How about meatloaf and instant potatoes?" I said, knowing it was the one meal I could concoct with minimal effort and out of ingredients right in my kitchen.

"That sounds lovely, my dear," she said, and then, pulling a small wooden box from her suitcase, she added, "And then we can play a game or two of dominos. Won't that be fun?"

"Fun" was not exactly how I would have described that Friday evening with Aunt Mae. Once the dishes were cleared away, she produced the domino tiles and treated me to a lengthy list of rules and exceptions before we began the game. And then, after we selected our tiles, my sweet, loving, accommodating Aunt Mae vanished, leaving in her place a fierce domino rival whose cutthroat approach made it clear that she had no intention of losing the game.

It was three a.m. before I could get her to put away the tiles and go to bed. If this was a typical evening with Aunt Mae, I thought before I drifted into an exhausted sleep, maybe it was a good thing that Freddie was coming. He could spell me the next time we played.

I was in the midst of a lengthy (and mostly one-sided) debate with Aunt Mae about the relative merits of barbecue chicken versus lasagna for dinner when Freddie finally put in an appearance Saturday at noon. He sauntered into the house like a long-awaited guest and asked, "Hey, cuz, what's going on? Got a place where I can catch some zzzs? It's been a long haul and I'm beat. Hungry, too," giving me a look that was supposed to convince me that death by starvation was imminent.

No "How nice to see you." No "Thanks for letting me stay." Freddie hadn't changed one bit, it seemed.

I sighed and led him to my bedroom-turned-home office-and-storage-room-turned-back-to-bedroom. After pushing my laptop to one side of my desk and stacking a week's worth of bills on top of it, I gestured in the general direction of the twin bed.

"There isn't much room, but after all, it's only for a few days," I said, hoping I made the hint strong enough, since I knew Freddie's tendency to take root wherever he landed.

Freddie plopped himself down on the bed, shoes and all, and promptly fell asleep, not bothering to express any gratitude for the accommodations. He also didn't bother to mention (and *why* did my family hold onto important details until the last possible moment?) that, sometime Sunday afternoon, his wife was coming—well, ex-wife really—along with her latest conquest *and* Baby Freddie.

"Oh, yeah, didn't I tell you that?" said Freddie, as he ate his third bowl of cereal the next morning. "Yeah, Sandy and what's-his-name," and he looked at his mother for help.

Aunt Mae stirred her coffee, looking as bright-eyed as though she had gone to bed at a reasonable hour, which she had most definitely not. I should know. I was right there with her to the bitter end of five rounds of dominos, lasting until the wee hours. If I never see a black tile with white dots again, it would be too soon.

"Charlie. His name is Charlie. And he's not good enough for her," Aunt Mae said, adding with a sidelong look at Freddie. "At least, not as good as you were, son. You treated that girl like gold!"

Well, if he *had*—a fact I doubted—it wasn't sufficient to make her stay. Sandy had only remained legally tied to Freddie long enough to bear him his son and namesake before rushing off to Vegas for a quickie divorce. But she was still invited to all the family functions. Indeed, Roberta had been foolish enough to make Baby Freddie her ring-bearer—a fact Sandy shared with me later that day when the three of them arrived.

"Isn't that wonderful?" she asked excitedly. "I just know he'll just be perfect, too!"

Huh, I thought to myself as I rearranged the sleeping plans. More likely he'll swallow the damned thing and then we'll have to spend the rest of the day trailing behind him every time he heads for the toilet. With a sigh, I booted Freddie to the living room sofa while assigning Sandy and her inamorata (aka, Charlie) the twin bed. The house was already bursting at the seams. If one more person came through the door with bag in hand, I was sure it would collapse like the walls of Jericho.

"It's a little narrow, isn't it?" Sandy said doubtfully when I had showed it to her, but then she giggled and turned to Charlie, saying "I'm sure we'll manage, won't we, honey?"

That was obviously my cue to leave unless I wanted a demonstration of how and what they would manage, which I most definitely did not. Besides, I was still left with Baby Freddie to place. He was too old for a crib, not that I had one handy since I hadn't yet embraced the joys of motherhood—or marital bliss, for that matter. The only solution was to push my bed against the wall and have him sleep on that side while I occupied the outside edge, serving as a human barricade. Not that I was concerned about him falling out of bed. It was more that I was worried about him making the rounds of my house while we were all sleeping.

Baby Freddie was a clever little boy, Sandy always said. In this case, clever meant he had learned to climb out of his crib at fourteen months, switch on the stove at two years, and lock Sandy out of the house numerous times before he turned three.

He had also figured out how to turn on the computer—a fact I discovered three o'clock Monday morning when I got up to use the bathroom and realized that the other side of the bed was absent its small occupant. It didn't take long to find him—the beeping noise and glowing light from the half-opened door to the spare room caught my attention. Averting my eyes from the bed and its entwined inhabitants, I pulled Baby Freddie's fingers from the keyboard and shut down the system, noticing with dismay that he had been "adjusting" the settings for the monitor display.

"No, no, NO!" he yelled, kicking my shins with unerring aim as I carried him back to the bedroom.

"Yes, yes, YES!" I said firmly and dumped him on my bed, tucking the blanket around him as tightly as I could and then taking my place next to him. If this routine kept up, I'd need a straitjacket—either for Baby Freddie or for myself.

Now the house was up to five uninvited guests—the maximum I believed it and I could handle. But as it turned out, I was wrong. The house, it seemed, could stretch to six, a fact I discovered when Uncle Carl, Aunt Mae's husband, showed up just a few hours later, his fist banging on my door with all the force of a Cat 5 hurricane.

"Who's here at this hour?" I muttered as I opened the door, only to be jolted fully awake by my uncle's booming voice asking, "Where's my girl?"

I noticed as I closed the door behind him (he hadn't waited for a formal invitation but took his welcome *and* permission to light up for granted) that he had parked his eighteen-wheeler in my narrow driveway, effectively blocking in my car and eliminating any opportunity for a quick escape.

"You might need to move your truck. And I'd really rather you didn't smoke in the house," I protested weakly, but my uncle overrode my objection, waving his cigar around while glowing ash dropped off the end and onto my couch and carpet.

"Nonsense, little girl! Why, a house without cigar smoke just doesn't smell right! This little stogie will give it a man's smell—just what a single girl like you needs!"

What *I* needed were less relatives invading my space, I thought as I went to get Aunt Mae, who could sleep through anything, even the thunderous voice of her beloved.

"By the way," Uncle Carl shouted as I headed down the hall, "do you have anything for Ellwood to eat?"

I stopped dead in my tracks. Ellwood? *Ellwood?* I searched my brain but couldn't recall any relative or relative-by-marriage with that name. And then the answer came to me—not as a bolt of lightning but as the vision of a skinny dachshund that was even now watering the scrawny Norfolk pine I had bought last week to serve as my Christmas tree.

"Damn it, boy!" Uncle Carl shouted. "I told you to go outside!"

He scooped up the animal while I detoured to the kitchen for some paper towels and water: the first in case Ellwood's aim was as bad as Freddie's was (if my toilet seat was any indication) and the second to dilute his "gift" before my pine died of urine overdose.

"Sorry, girl," Uncle Carl said, holding the wriggling Ellwood under his arm like an oversized sausage. "I'll just lock him in the kitchen for now. He's used to cramped quarters."

My kitchen isn't cramped, I thought resentfully. It just wasn't made for six uninvited people and one unhousebroken canine.

"What's for breakfast, cousin?" asked Freddie, ambling into the room an hour later while I tried to dodge the dog's rope leash.

"For God's sake, Freddie!" I said in exasperation. "Can't you see I've got my hands full? Find something and eat it!"

Bad advice, it turned out, as the leftover meatloaf I had earmarked for lunch disappeared in Freddie's mouth. At this rate, my entire monthly food budget would be gone in a week.

"Thanks, kid," said Freddie, dropping his empty dish onto the counter. "Hey, isn't Sandy up yet?" he asked, as he headed toward the door.

I shook my head and then, as the pitter-patter of Baby Freddie's feet announced his arrival, I decided to wake up the other person responsible for that walking, talking force of destruction. At first, I tapped lightly on the door, but when that brought no response, I banged on it, before pushing the door open in exasperation.

"Oh, no!" my eyes taking in the empty bed and scrawled note pinned to the lampshade.

"Dear Cassie, Charlie and I are off for a few days to the Dew Drop Inn. Your house is just too crowded, if you know what I mean! We'll be back Wednesday morning in time to get Baby Freddie ready for the wedding."

Sandy had signed the note with the letter "S" surrounded by a smiley face—her concept of the emotion the note would create. But I had never felt less like smiling. I rushed back to the kitchen, narrowly missing Aunt Mae who was coming in to brew more fresh coffee for "her man" but I was too late. Freddie was already gone.

"Damn it!" I said, and then, as I watched Aunt Mae pour what was left of the coffee down the drain, "What are you doing? I just made that pot!"

She shook her head. "Carl likes his coffee fresh-brewed and strong, dear," she explained, ladling spoon after spoon of coffee into the brew basket.

No wonder he was able to drive as much as he did, I thought. With that much caffeine, he could probably go coast-to-coast without any sleep at all.

"You seem tense, dear. Is something wrong?"

I pulled Ellwood's head out of the wastebasket before dropping onto a chair to drink the now cold liquid in my coffee cup. I had poured my coffee an hour ago, but what with the dog and Freddie, I hadn't had much chance to enjoy it.

"No, not unless you count Sandy taking off and sticking us with the kid," I said, watching Baby Freddie out of the corner of my eye. He and Ellwood were both eyeing the dog treats that Uncle Carl left on the counter, and I decided that I didn't care which one of them got to the box first.

"Why, I think that is so romantic!" Aunt Mae rhapsodized as her husband came into the room. "Carl, don't you think it's romantic?"

But Uncle Carl just grunted, looked over at the pot meaningfully and then sat down with the latest issue of *Trucker's World Magazine*.

"Why don't you ever take me away for the week, Carl?" Aunt Mae continued.

But at that point, I needed to get the conversation back to the problem at hand, who was even now taking apart the television remote control. "I can't baby-sit Baby Freddie, Aunt Mae. I don't know anything about kids and besides, I have things to do. This was supposed to be my vacation and—"

"Every woman knows enough about kids to watch them for a day," Uncle Carl said, taking the coffee Aunt Mae had poured for him before heading to the living room. "Besides, how much trouble could one kid get into?"

This was something I devoutly did not want to find out. But short of locking him in the garage (an idea to which I gave more than just passing consideration), I didn't know what to do. I couldn't very well drag Sandy back. And putting Freddie in charge of his progeny was a recipe for disaster. No, I was stuck with Baby Freddie along with the rest of my relatives, and there wasn't anything I could do about it. I buried my head in my hands.

"Mae! Where are you, Mae? I got a load of laundry here with your name on it!" Carl's voice echoed in the kitchen.

Aunt Mae hurriedly set her coffee cup down as though it burned her fingers and answered, "I'm coming, Carl!" before turning to me. "I'll just wash his clothes and then we can start planning dinner, Cassie. Think how nice it will be—all of us together at the table enjoying a meal!"

Meal, I said to myself. That meant food, which meant I needed to get to the store ASAP if we were going to have dinner at all. Room spray, too, I added to my mental shopping list as the clouds of cigar smoke drifted out from the living room. *And ash trays, before my carpets get any more burn holes.*

But first, I had to find the two youngest inhabitants, who had disappeared from the kitchen and were undoubtedly getting into things they shouldn't. Just two more days to the wedding, I kept repeating to myself, as I hauled Baby Freddie and then Ellwood out of the toilet bowl (the first one engaged in dumping in wads of toilet paper and the second in satisfying his interminable thirst), before getting Uncle Carl to move his truck, and Aunt Mae to watch everyone else, so I could run to the store.

Two more days—but they seemed like two hundred, I thought as I drove to Big Bob's Foods. I didn't even have the relief of going to work—not that I would want to leave my house at the mercy of my relatives. I sighed, thinking of the plans I had made for my holiday break: balance my checkbook, sort out the kitchen cabinets, maybe even put up a holiday decoration or two. In any case, none of them involved feeding and cleaning up after a boatload of relatives. But so far, I had spent my vacation grocery shopping, cooking, and playing dominoes—and hoping against hope that Roberta's wedding would be cancelled, and everyone would leave before I lost my manners or my mind.

I marched through the grocery aisles, muttering to myself like an escapee from a padded cell. "I didn't ask for this. This is too much. And leaving the kid behind without even asking," a refrain that continued until I returned home. Predictably, Freddie showed up after I carried all eight bags into the house and had started stowing the groceries in the refrigerator and cupboard.

He reached out for a bag of chips but then dropped his outstretched hand back to his side when I barked, "Don't touch anything!"

"I wasn't going to eat anything. I just wanted to look," he said in a hurt voice, but one glance at my face and he gave up any pretense of innocence and changed the subject. "What's with your car? It's missing," casually helping himself to a cookie from a package I swore hadn't been open before he came in the room.

"What do you mean?" I asked in alarm. I took a quick look out the window. No, it was there and as far as I could tell, it still had four wheels and all the doors, even if the lock worked on only one of them. "'Missing'? What do you mean, 'missing'?"

"When's the last time you had a tune-up?" he answered, the pitying tone in his voice making it clear that he thought my vehicle knowledge left much to be desired.

"Me? Oh, you mean, my car. Well, I had the oil changed last spring, I think," but he shook his head.

130

"A tune-up," dragging the words out as though he was speaking to someone for whom English was a second language. "I think your car needs some work."

I recognized the sound of excitement in his tone. I had heard it in other men's voices as well, unfortunately rarely in connection with me. It was the car thing again. But I didn't want Freddie to mess with it. I didn't know if he knew what he was doing or if he even knew a distributor from a carburetor— not that I did either, but I *had* heard the terms.

"Don't—" but it was too late. Freddie lured Uncle Carl from the couch where he was watching NASCAR reruns with the magic words "car problems." For the next several hours, my poor vehicle had to endure the poking and prodding of four hands, not to mention the draining of gallons of black, green and red fluids *and* a removal-and-replacement of every part in the engine compartment, with periodic runs around the block so the two mechanics (and I use the term loosely) could judge its performance and their expertise.

In the meantime, I was stuck with the kid, and it only took me about half an hour to realize I was in over my head. I considered taking him for a walk but knowing how fast he could run, decided against that strategy. For an all-too-brief time, I occupied him with stacking the canned goods from my pantry into a barricade, but that lasted only until he figured out it was more fun to throw them, barely missing Ellwood *and* my kitchen window *and* me in the process.

"Aunt Mae, help me out here," I begged in desperation, interrupting her hourly "coiffure check." Every morning by nine a.m., Aunt Mae could be found in front of the mirror, backcombing and spraying her dyed hair into a style that resembled a frosted helmet. The rest of the day was spent checking its condition, making sure every hair was still in place.

"Don't you have any crayons? Storybooks? Playing cards?"

To each question, I could only shake my head. Obviously, I was woefully unprepared for child-rearing or even baby-sitting.

"Never mind," she said, and I wasn't sure which one of us she was comforting. "I'll find something."

She darted into the bedroom from which Sandy had recently escaped, rummaging through the drawers until she found some pens and printer paper.

"Come on, Freddie, you and I will draw pictures at the table," and amazingly enough, the little twerp followed her to the kitchen like a well-trained dog, leaving me feeling like a total failure. I brought up the rear and sat at the table watching them for the next hour, unsure how long the art class would occupy Baby Freddie and what I should be doing while it was going on. The slamming of the car hood solved that problem. Uncle Carl came in, followed by Freddie, who wiped his grease-stained hands on my kitchen towel before turning to me.

"Car's almost done. We'll finish it after we eat. Got any beer? What's for supper?"

I pulled a box of macaroni and cheese from the cabinet and handed my cousin a carton of matches. "Light the grill. It's hot dogs tonight," I said

The hell with fat, sodium, and cholesterol. Dogs were fast, cheap, and required minimal clean-up—my kind of meal. And everyone else's as well, since the two packages vanished along with the twelve-pack of beer that had magically appeared in my refrigerator.

By the time I cleaned up the kitchen, the men were back at my vehicle, and I decided not to ask what they were doing. Whatever it was, it involved a fair bit of noise and more than a few swear words. The work kept them occupied until well past nine, when they finally came in, pronounced the car good as new, and then took themselves into the living room to watch yet another race car rerun while Aunt Mae was bathing Baby Freddie.

"Thanks for doing the car," I said, but both men just waved their hands, their eyes never leaving the set.

"No biggee," said Freddie. "After all, you don't have anyone to help you out."

For a minute, the feminist side of me wanted to retort that I didn't *need* anybody, but if that was true, then my car would have had its tune-up (and God knows what else) when it needed it—which, according to the men, was about ten thousand miles ago. But I let it go and went to my bedroom to find Aunt Mae telling my roomie a bedtime story. Baby Freddie's determination to stay awake was fighting a losing battle with his body's need for sleep, and I watched in fascination as his eyelids drooped and then snapped open again until finally gravity and tiredness won.

"He's asleep now," Aunt Mae whispered, slipping off the bed before turning to look critically at me. "You look like you need sleep too, my dear," and for a minute I thought she was going to offer to read me a story as well. But she only gave me a quick hug before leaving the room. I crawled wearily into my side of the bed, lulled to sleep by the steady breathing of Baby Freddie and the muted roar of the men cheering as the various cars pulled into the lead.

The next morning, I awoke in a surprisingly good mood—which lasted only until I came face to face with the wreckage that once was my relatively neat living room. Empty cans of beer, empty bags of chips and definitely *not* empty ashtrays were scattered throughout the room. The men had either celebrated their favorite driver winning the race or drowned their sorrows at his loss—I wasn't sure which and didn't much care. All I wanted was to get the living room cleaned up so I could have my morning cup of coffee in peace. Wishful thinking, as it turned out.

I had finished returning the living room to its pre-relative state and was pouring my first cup of caffeine when Freddie came into the kitchen.

"What's for breakfast?" he asked, randomly opening cabinets and drawers as though food would just magically appear.

Remembering his work on my car, I held back a sharp retort before answering, "I have toast and"—after a quick look inside the refrigerator—"well, just toast, I guess" resignedly adding "eggs" to the grocery list. Last Thursday, I had two dozen. Less than a week later, there were none. Somehow in the space of five days, all twenty-four had vanished.

"No bacon? Sausage? How about some corned beef hash?" he said hopefully but, after a look at my face, he must have thought the better of continuing the conversation and instead opted for a long gulp of orange juice, straight from the carton.

"Freddie, for God's sakes, I have glasses!" I said, but he just shrugged his shoulders, and I decided to drop the issue. Besides, I had to resolve a more pressing problem. My two o'clock shampoo-and-trim was coming up fast, and I didn't know what to do with everybody. And then there was Ellwood, who had displayed his contempt for my kitchen by chewing the corners of every cabinet door his stumpy legs would let him reach.

The only solution, not that I had much faith in the results, was to leave Aunt Mae in charge. But like everything else that had been happening during the past few days, my idea didn't turn out the way I hoped.

"Aunt Mae," I began, when I finally tracked her down on the back porch, where she was sitting with Uncle Carl, "I have a hair appointment this afternoon and I was wondering—"

But that was as far as I got before Aunt Mae interrupted me. "Why, Cassie, how sweet of you to ask and of course I'd love to go with you! Carl, you don't mind if I go with her, do you?"

"Of course not, sweetheart!" he answered, and then reached into his back pocket to pull out his overstuffed wallet. He took out a wad of twenties and handed them over to her. "Here, this is for the two of you. Now run along and get prettied up!"

This put me between the proverbial rock and hard place. I *could* explain to Aunt Mae that what I really wanted was for her to ride herd on the three males—four, if you count Ellwood—until I got back, but one look at her beaming face and I didn't have the heart to say it. Besides, given that I had to make yet another grocery run to tide us over for the next two days, having someone else foot the bill for my haircut was more than welcome.

"Uh, sure, as long as Uncle Carl and Freddie can keep an eye on the kid and the dog," I said. "When I get back from buying groceries, we'll leave for the salon."

In record time, I went to the store, returned home, and put away the food, stopping only long enough to give clear orders to Freddie to keep out of the pantry, refrigerator, and freezer, and to Uncle Carl to keep an eye on both Freddies. Then Aunt Mae and I headed to Klip-N-Kurl. But if I hoped Aunt Mae would be quiet while she was getting her hair done, that thought was dashed, since she was barely seated at the shampoo station before she started.

"My niece Cassie is so sweet! You know, she invited our whole family to stay with her when we came to town for Roberta's wedding! Roberta's my other niece," she continued, while the shampoo girl did her best to get the layers of hairspray out of Aunt Mae's locks. "She's marrying a podiatrist and they are going on a cruise for their honeymoon. Isn't that romantic? Now, poor Cassie here, she's never been married, but it isn't because she's not a good girl. She just doesn't do enough with herself to attract men!"

I wanted to dispute her statement, since after all, I *had* had my share of dates—well, a small share anyway, although the last one's idea of a "classy evening" was the two-for-one special at the Blue Plate Truck Stop. As for my appearance, how dressed up should I be to work in a school cafeteria? But then I caught sight of my reflection: hair pulled back, no make-up, dressed in a sweatshirt and jeans, both bearing stains from the last time I had painted the porch. Even Aunt Mae, for all her overdone makeup and teased hair, looked more presentable than I did.

"Well, Cassie, do you want the same as always?" asked Mary Ellen, standing behind me.

I looked over at Aunt Mae, now seated next to me with her head swathed in a towel, and her encouraging smile combined with the recollection of the wad of twenties donated by Uncle Carl was enough to change my mind.

"Nope, give me the works, Mary Ellen!"—dangerous words to be spoken to anyone with scissors and bottles of chemicals at her disposal.

Several hours later, the mirror reflected a new me—well, to be totally accurate, it was the same me, only better. Mary Ellen had chopped off about five inches of split ends and then highlighted my mousy brown shade with something called "Desert Sand." The nails on my fingers and toes were flashing "Stop Light Red" while my cheeks tingled from the combined attack of an exfoliant scrub and facial massage.

"Why Cassie, you look lovely!" Aunt Mae said when I got up from the chair and impulsively I gave her a hug.

"Thanks, Aunt Mae! And you look terrific, too," I added belatedly, and on the whole she did. Her hair was less lacquered and the cut she got made her seem, if not ten years younger, at least not quite her age. "Now we better get home so I can come up with something for dinner."

But when I turned the corner and saw the front of my house, my concern about what I was going to feed everybody was pushed aside. At least, I *thought* it was my house, although it didn't look a bit like the place I had left just a few hours earlier. Every square inch of the exterior was covered with blinking red and green lights, while on the roof, Santa was sitting, not in the traditional sleigh, but astride a motorcycle.

"What the heck happened here?"

"Pretty cool, right, cousin?" said Freddie, as I sat there dumbfounded in the driveway. "We thought the place needed to get into the spirit of the season, so Dad and I cleaned out the stores of all their holiday crap. Wait until you see the inside!"

I followed him into my house, where every available flat surface featured some kind of holiday item, from a ceramic tree whose base doubled as an ashtray (already overflowing) to the toilet seat that played "Jingle Bells" every time the lid was lifted.

I didn't know what to say, so settled for a weak "Thanks but you shouldn't have," resisting the urge to add, "And I wish you hadn't" since their intentions were good, if more than a little overdone.

"Oh, Carl, it's lovely!" said Aunt Mae, making up for my lack of enthusiasm.

"Not as lovely as you, sweetheart," said Uncle Carl with a sidelong glance at his wife. "Tell you what, little girl," looking over at me, "how about you and the missus get all gussied up—not that you aren't already a real looker, honey," and Aunt Mae blushed like a teenager, "and then we'll all go out to eat. On me. What do you say, Cassie? That way you don't have to mess up your fancy manicure."

"Why, Carl, what a great idea!" said Aunt Mae before I could answer, grabbing my arm and dragging me down the hall. "Let's hurry up, Cassie. The men want to eat!"

It didn't take long for the two of us to change our clothes, but once at the door, I realized that after we were gone, Ellwood would be left to his own devices. I considered my options for his placement: the basement, the garage or, as a last and not completely unappealing resort, the dog pound. But I decided that the last one, tempting as it was, might be going a bit too far, and settled for tying him to the front porch banister that I hoped would be strong enough to hold him until we returned.

Then, once everyone was squashed in my little car, I put it in reverse, automatically looking at the gas gauge where I expected to see the needle hovering in the less-than-a-quarter-tank sector. But instead, it was firmly positioned at full. I tapped the gauge, but nothing changed.

"Oh, yeah, I filled the tank up while you were getting changed," said Uncle Carl. "You know, you shouldn't let it get so low. You never know when you might need to take off in an emergency."

Like when your relatives show up without warning, was my first uncharitable thought, but instead said, "Well, thanks. That was really sweet of you."

Then Freddie leaned forward and tapped me on the shoulder. "Did you notice that the warning light on the dash isn't flashing anymore? We fixed it!" he said proudly.

I wanted to ask if by "fix it" he meant they had dealt with the problem or simply disconnected the wire that lit the bulb but settled for another thank you.

Then Uncle Carl said, "Sit back, boy, so we can get going! I'm in the mood for spaghetti and meatballs! Where are you taking us, Cassie?"

"Well, the closest place is Leo's Ristorante," I answered. "It's known for an all-you-can-eat Italian buffet. How does that sound?"

Not surprisingly, it was met with agreement from everyone, and I breathed a sigh of relief, hoping we could get in and out before Ellwood destroyed my porch. Once inside the restaurant, Tina, our waitress, started us off with breadsticks and butter, and from that point on, kept us supplied with coffee (for me and Aunt Mae), beer (for the men) and milk (for the kid). She also laughed at Uncle Carl's jokes, flirted shamelessly with Freddie, complimented Aunt Mae on her hair, outfit and shoes, and charmed Baby Freddie into eating with a kid-sized fork.

I watched her in awe and wondered how she managed to stay so cheerful and upbeat when faced with a crowd like my relatives who plowed through everything in record time, not to mention Bay Freddie who had just spilled his third glass of milk.

"He's not mine," I said apologetically as she wiped up the table and his booster chair. "My relatives are only in town for a family wedding, and they'll be leaving in two days. As for Baby Freddie's mother…" trailing off at that point, since I didn't want to get into the whole Sandy-Charlie-Freddie backstory.

"No problem," she said, waving her hand. "I've got three younger brothers, so I know what it's like. Just enjoy your time with your family while they're here."

Maybe that was the secret, I thought later, when I was sitting outside on my porch while Aunt Mae was putting Baby Freddie to bed. Instead of looking at all those admittedly irritating things my relatives did, I should just relax and let it go. After all, it wasn't liked they *lived* with me. Plus, the wedding was tomorrow, and by Thursday afternoon, they should all be out of my place and on the road, leaving me all by myself in my quiet house on the day before Christmas. In my quiet, *empty* house, surrounded by all the holiday décor my cousin and uncle had bought me, with no one to celebrate with. No spouse. No kids. Not even my parents, since by now they would be in Nassau where my mother would buy every little trinket she could find that had "Welcome to The Bahamas" on it, even if they were all made in China.

I put my feet up on the railing, noticing that, unlike a few days ago, it didn't wobble under the weight. I had been meaning to fix the supports, but never got around to it. But clearly someone had—probably Uncle Carl, whose toolbox rivaled the hardware store. He never said anything about doing that either, or about replacing the burnt-out bulb in the yard light that I saw was now glowing nicely. He just fixed them without making a big deal about it.

Unlike me, I realized, who made a big deal out of everything. While I couldn't deny that it had been a little challenging to housekeep for unexpected guests, it hadn't been as bad as I feared. In their own way, Uncle Carl and Aunt Mae had been sweet, and the Freddies—well, they weren't as awful as they could have been, even if their table manners left more than a little to be desired.

The screen door squeaked open, and Freddie stuck out his head. "Okay if I come out?" he asked, and I nodded. He pulled up a chair, lit a cigarette and popped the tab off his can of beer, flipping it to the floor and then, after catching my eye, sheepishly retrieving it from where it had landed.

"Look, thanks for putting us up and all," he said. "I know you weren't expecting company, and my kid can be a handful."

I waved away his words, the two glasses of red wine I had had with dinner no doubt contributing to my feeling of charity and expansiveness. "No big deal," I said. I reached over to take a swig from his can before handing it back, and then leaned my head back against the chair. "We're family, after all," a fact that had escaped me until that moment.

The silence stretched out as I cast around for a conversational topic before settling on baseball. "So, what do you think of the Mets?"

We spent the next hour or two in desultory conversation: who would win the World Series (he was a diehard Mets fan while I favored the Yankees), why my car sputtered on cold mornings (he said it was probably a dirty carburetor and offered to run some cleaner through it in the morning), and whether Sandy would come back (to the house or to him, neither one of us was sure since the fourth can of beer on top of all the wine we'd had was making both of us a little fuzzy). I've no idea what time we called it a night, but I'm sure it was well past one when Freddie hit the couch and I stumbled to my side of the bed, trying not to wake the kid.

Wednesday morning dawned bright and clear, which was more than I could say for myself. I wasn't used to drinking, and the beer and wine (especially in the amount I had imbibed) was a lethal combination for both my head and stomach. I collided with Uncle Carl outside the bathroom door, but, after taking one look at my face, he apparently decided his normal tone was more than I could handle.

"Looks like you and Freddie made a late night of it," he said, his voice slightly lower than usual, which was still loud enough to make my head throb. "What you need is a good breakfast of ham and eggs to get you ready for the wedding!"

Just the thought of it was enough to make my stomach turn. Besides, I wasn't up to doing anything that required more energy than brewing a pot of coffee. I waved my hand and escaped into the bathroom, where I spent the next fifteen minutes in the shower, hoping that the steam and hot water would make the pounding in my head go away. And it probably would have, except for the repeated interruptions: first Freddie ("Are you almost done?"), then Aunt Mae ("I don't mean to bother you, but Carl needs to shave.") and finally Baby Freddie who, judging by the sound, was using a wooden spoon to bang on the door.

I gave up, got out of the shower, and went to my room to get ready for the wedding. Luckily, Sandy and Charlie showed up on time to get Baby Freddie dressed and out the door, and the rest of us followed—Aunt Mae and Uncle Carl in Freddie's truck and me bringing up the rear in my car.

The next few hours were taken up with the nuptials, during which (surprising everyone) Baby Freddie kept the ring out of his mouth long enough for the hapless groom to place it on his bride's finger. Next came the bridal luncheon at Big Mac's Cafeteria, during which (surprising no one) Baby Freddie managed to get to the cake and pull off a chunk big enough to send the next tier cascading toward the tabletop.

"No, no, it's all good!" yelled my cousin, grabbing his son with one hand while he shoved the section back in place. Then Freddie ruined his save by licking the frosting from his palm, adding, "Hmmm, it really *is* good."

Then, once the guests had enough of the food, the party moved to the back parking lot for the dancing part of the reception. Freddie cranked up his sound system in his pickup and soon the surrounding neighborhood was treated to a selection of country songs chosen by my cousin for the event. Pretty soon, everybody from Baby Freddie to the senior members of the group were kicking up their heels on the asphalt to George Jones, Tammy Wynette, Johnny Cash, and Dolly Parton, only pausing long enough to hit the ice chest of beer and wine coolers Freddie had thoughtfully stored in the bed of his truck.

Since my head was still feeling the effects of the alcohol from the night before, I settled myself as far away as possible from the noise emanating from Freddie's truck and reflected on the past few days. Stressful? Without a doubt. Aggravating at times? You betcha. But it wasn't all bad, I had to admit. Uncle Carl and Freddie *had* fixed my car and decorated my house, and it was kind of fun to plan meals with Aunt Mae. Even feeling

Baby Freddie's body against me all night long was in some bizarre way almost enjoyable—at least as long as he wasn't kicking me.

Well, by tomorrow afternoon, I'd have my house and my life back—just in time for the holidays. I could restock my kitchen with organic peanut butter and vanilla creamer, grab a couple more bagels from Mrs. Schatskie's Deli before she shut down for two days, and relax in the peace and quiet of my four walls to await Ol' Saint Nick.

All by myself. All alone. On what was supposed to be the ultimate family holiday of the year.

Just then, "Tennessee Waltz" came on, followed by "Could I Have This Dance." Uncle Carl led Aunt Mae out onto the lot, where he dipped and twirled her through both songs while she looked up at him with adoring eyes. I had to admit that watching those two sixty-year-olds dancing like teenagers in love, got me more than a little choked up.

But before my emotions got the better of me—and what's up with *that*, I asked myself—Freddie put on the closing song: "This Is It" by Kenny Loggins, not exactly my choice for a wedding reception, but then, that was Freddie. Then, before I knew what was happening, he was hauling my butt out onto the asphalt, and I was dancing with my cousin like a teenager myself.

"Wow, way to go, cuz!" he said when the song ended as I held onto his shoulder and tried to catch my breath.

"Not bad yourself," I gasped, and then Uncle Carl with Baby Freddie on his shoulders and Aunt Mae with her hair every which way came up to the two of us, and for a brief moment, we stood there like we were waiting for someone to take our picture.

"I'm going to miss you guys," I blurted out, and Uncle Carl beamed while Aunt Mae's eyes grew suspiciously bright.

"Oh, honey, we're going to miss you, too," she said and at that moment, Baby Freddie slid down Uncle Carl's back and ran over to give my legs a sticky hug.

"I *wuv* Aunt Cassie!" he declared.

And in retrospect, that was what did it. How else to explain the next words that came out of my mouth? "Why don't you all stay and have Christmas with me? We're family, after all!"

Mistletoe Magic

"Welcome to Baxter's!"

Susan knew her voice was hardly as cheery as it should be as she greeted the couple entering the store, but she couldn't help it. More people. And there were bound to be other customers as well. Everybody waited until Christmas Eve to get their last-minute items, it seemed. And she *still* had an hour before closing time, which seemed like an eternity. She couldn't wait until she could go home, lie down on the couch, and try to convince the baby to just stay still and wait for Brandon to come home.

"I really would prefer that you stopped working," her obstetrician had told her three weeks ago. "The baby could come at any time, and the last thing you need to do is to be out in the snow and ice where you might fall. Or around customers where you might catch the flu. Or go into labor at the store. Or—"

But Susan interrupted her, doing her best to sound positive and decisive. "I'll be fine. After all, the baby isn't due yet. And my last day is Christmas Eve. Then I promise to stop. And by then my husband will be home and—"

But there Susan stopped. She didn't *know* when Brandon would be home. Even *he* didn't know. When she wrote him last spring to tell him she was pregnant, he promised he'd be back in time for the birth. But the Army didn't care what he promised or what she wanted, she told herself now. When you enlisted, you knew that they owned you, body and soul, and you went *where* they sent you *when* they sent you, and that was that.

"Have you heard from your husband?" Dr. Adams had asked, but Susan just shook her head. "Well, even if he isn't here when the baby is born, you won't be alone. The hospital is wonderful. The nurses are used to military wives coming in without their spouses, and the staff will do their best to take care of you. In the meantime," she added as she helped Susan down from the examination table, "if you have any questions or concerns, just call the office. Okay?"

Susan nodded, but the only real question she had was when Brandon was coming home, and no one—not even the doctor, nice as she was—could answer that. So, all Susan could do while she waited was to come to Baxter's and work her evening shifts and then go home to her empty bed, hoping each night that Brandon would be there when she awoke.

But it hadn't happened, and here she was on Christmas Eve, doing her best not to think about where her husband might be and whether he was safe. And when she would see him again.

If she would see him again.

Maggie pulled her coat collar closer around her neck. If she had known how strong the wind was, she never would have come out. And she wouldn't have needed to if she had checked the refrigerator before placing her grocery order last Saturday. Then cream would have been on the list. Instead, here she was,

NANCY CHRISTIE

risking life and limb on Christmas Eve to go to the nearby convenience store.

All because she couldn't drink her coffee black, like Matthew does. Like Matthew *did*.

"You need to pay better attention, my girl," she said aloud, and then flushed when the couple ahead of her turned and gave her a quick glance before entering the shop where Maggie was headed.

She never used to talk to herself. There was no need, not when she had Matthew to talk to. But now he was gone and talking to herself was one indication of how her life had changed since last spring. Like the habit she had fallen into of spending nights on the couch instead of being in the bed they had shared for more than sixty years. And the kinds of suppers she ate now, usually canned soup and crackers rather than the big dinners of meat and potatoes and vegetables she had once cooked for Matthew.

If Alix knew her mother was out on the icy streets after dark, she'd have a fit, Maggie thought. She'd say it was just another example of why Maggie should come live with them instead of staying alone in the empty house. And that's the topic Alix would focus on if Maggie were to spend Christmas with her, Maggie knew, which was her main reason for declining her daughter's holiday invitation. Alix had even brought it up again during their most recent phone conversation.

"You can't stay there all alone, Mom. Dad is gone and I know you miss him, but if you come here, you'll see how nice it is. The weather is warm, and you wouldn't have to worry about cooking or cleaning or shopping. At least come for Christmas. Jenny is coming with the baby—your first great-grandchild!" she added, with the wheedling tone that, as a child, she had used successfully on her father to get her way. "It's Nathan's first Christmas, after all. Don't you want to be here for that?"

But Maggie was not as easy to win over as Matthew had been. "There will be other Christmases with Nathan," she said, and then, aware that her daughter might take that to mean Maggie didn't care at all about the baby, she added, "But I'll call you all Christmas morning first thing when I wake up and you can put him on the phone so I can talk to him. I'm usually up at seven, you know."

"But Mom, that's four o'clock here in Los Angeles, remember? We'll still be sleeping!" and Maggie could hear the unspoken thoughts in her daughter's voice: *Mom is losing it. She forgot about the time difference. She probably forgets to take her meds, too. We'll have to move her whether she wants to come or not.*

And Maggie didn't want to—not yet anyway. Although there were times, like tonight, for instance, when she thought how much easier it would be if she lived with Alix in that comfortable spare bedroom on the first floor. No stairs to climb, no laundry to do, no meals to prepare. And no cold weather to deal with, either, although Maggie liked watching the snow fall to blanket the trees and lawn. It brought back memories of that night long ago when she first met Matthew. It was at a New Year's Eve party, and afterward, he had walked her home through the falling snow and then gently kissed the flakes from her lashes and cheeks before touching her cold lips with his warm mouth.

Maybe someday she'd decide to move to California. But not now. She couldn't bear to leave the house where she had lived for so long.

Alix thought the house was empty. But she was wrong. Matthew was still there, in every room.

"Damn it, Jack, why didn't you tell me sooner?"

"I know. I'm sorry." Jack reached for his wife's hand, but she pulled away. She did that a lot these days, he realized. It was as though, with the last failed attempt to have a baby, she didn't want to have anything to do with him at all anymore.

"All the tests show that both of you are in good shape as far as the ability to get pregnant," the specialist had told them two years ago. So dutifully, they had tried monitoring Denise's ovulation periods, tracking temperatures, even using different positions in case one of them might do the trick. But after so many months of disappointment, they gradually stopped making the effort.

And stopped touching. And stopped talking—really talking. Now, the only time Denise spoke to him was when she had to and always with a sharpness in her voice that hadn't been there before. Sometimes Jack wondered if they would be better off calling it quits. Sometimes he wondered if, despite what the doctor had said, he was the one who was at fault. And sometimes, all he wanted was to hold his wife and tell her that it didn't matter, that even if they didn't have a baby, they still had each other.

"Just wait here and I'll find something," Denise said and stalked off, leaving Jack standing by the register.

"Are you looking for something special?" asked the store clerk.

"No. Well, maybe yes. I mean, my wife is looking for a kid's toy for a donation. She went down that aisle," Jack said, pointing to the left. "You do have toys, right?"

She nodded. "I'll just go help her, shall I?" And she headed in the direction he had indicated, walking in the slightly off-balance gait that all women had near the end of their pregnancies.

Jack watched her leave, hoping the clerk could help his wife find something suitable and they could get on their way. They were already late for his boss's holiday party—first because he had to stop and buy gas and then because he had forgotten about the gift they were supposed to bring until they were almost there.

Last year it was canned goods for the local food pantry, but this year his boss's wife had asked for toys for the homeless shelter—the worst possible item for Jack and Denise to have to shop for, especially since Denise's period had started the day before. Not that there was any chance of her being pregnant anyway. It had been so long since they'd made love that he didn't even remember the last time they'd done it.

Just for a moment, he wondered what it would have been like if, this Christmas, Denise were to be having a baby. A child. *Their* child. He had been thinking for so long in terms of Denise's getting pregnant that he hadn't really thought about what it would be like to be a family, to have a baby together. A son or a daughter—Jack didn't care which it was. All he knew was that he wanted a child with Denise. But even if that didn't happen, he knew he still wanted to be with Denise.

He only hoped it was not too late.

###

Carol hated bringing her son out in this weather, but it couldn't be helped. If the sitter had called before Carol left work to tell her there was no more juice, then she could have bought it on her way home. But she hadn't, and Carol didn't want to make a fuss. Sitters were hard enough to find, and at least this one didn't ask for more money than Carol could afford. She barely had enough as it was after paying the bills.

She had counted on her holiday bonus to buy Joey a present or two. But then her boss appeared on the factory floor to make an unexpected announcement just before he left on his annual two-week holiday cruise.

"This has been a lean year for all of us, so I'm afraid Santa won't be bringing anything extra in your paychecks. But I hope you enjoy your Christmas, and I'll see you all here after the New Year. Merry Christmas, everybody!"

"Merry Christmas," everyone responded dutifully before heading back to their workstations. But Carol just stood there, wondering how she would tell her son that Santa wasn't coming this year. It was bad enough that Joey wasn't feeling well. She knew that bringing him out in the cold was a bad idea, but she couldn't leave him home alone and hoped that the juice might help him. At least they could get on the bus close to their apartment, and the first stop was at the corner right by the convenience store.

"It will just take me a minute, honey," she'd said, bundling him up. "I'll get your juice and a few more things and then we can go right back home. Okay?"

He was a good boy, she knew. He never complained—not when they had peanut butter sandwiches night after night, not when he had to wear clothes from the secondhand store, not when he had to eat school lunches set aside for the kids who couldn't afford to buy what they wanted. That made it all the harder for her when he asked, just as they came into Baxter's, if he could buy a toy.

"Just a little one, please, Mommy? Just in case Santa doesn't come again this year."

Carol flushed, knowing the man standing by the register counter had overhead what her son said. By the looks of his coat and shoes, he certainly would be able to buy his kids anything they wanted, she thought resentfully, while she had to watch every penny just so she could keep the lights and heat on and feed her son.

"We'll see, honey," she said, mentally calculating what she had to buy against the money in her wallet. "Now you wait here, and I'll be right back, okay?" And she gave her son a quick hug.

Just for a moment, Carol wondered if it would always be like this or if, someday, she would have enough money to give her son what he needed and what he wanted.

But right now, all she had to give him was love.

Maggie shivered as sleet needles stabbed her face. Thank God Baxter's was right around the corner from her house. She pulled open the heavy door, hearing the chime as she did so, and stepped through the entrance, intending to get the cream she needed and go back home. But once inside, the lure of all the holiday decorations pulled at her, and she began to walk the aisles, stopping to finger the tinsel garland, stroke the soft fur cuff on the Christmas stockings, and wind up the musical sleigh so it would play "Santa Claus Is Comin' to Town."

Then on a nearby table she spotted a small display of mistletoe ornaments, each with a tiny silver bell. She lifted one into the air and shook it, just to hear the delicate tinkle it made.

"How pretty that is!"

Maggie turned to see who had spoken. It was a young woman, a tired young woman, she realized, with dark circles under her eyes and a drawn look to her face.

"Yes, it is, but not at all what I came here for," Maggie answered with a smile. "I ran out of cream, and I just can't bring myself to drink coffee without it. So here I am on Christmas Eve, doing some last-minute shopping."

Reluctantly, she set the ornament back on the table and turned toward the cold-food section, the young woman falling into step with her until they both stopped in front of the juice and dairy products. Maggie reached for her cream at the same time the woman picked up a carton of brand-name orange juice, but then, after reading the shelf tag, set it back.

"Too expensive," she murmured, taking the store brand instead. "Everything costs so much," she added, glancing over at Maggie who smiled sympathetically. "I wouldn't have even come out tonight except my son has a sore throat and he wanted some orange juice, so here we are," and she nodded toward the front of the store where Maggie glimpsed a little boy waiting patiently.

"Well, I hope he feels better soon. That's no way to celebrate Christmas," Maggie said, adding, "And I wish you both a very nice holiday!"

But the woman just gave her a half-smile in response as though a nice holiday were something only to be wished for but never achieved.

"Well, I'd best be going before the weather gets any worse," Maggie said and then started toward the register, noting with disappointment as she passed the small table that the mistletoe ornaments were no longer there.

I didn't need one anyway, she thought, but still she wished she had bought one. Their first Christmas together, Matthew had hung a mistletoe ball in the hallway. From that day on, each night on their way to bed, Matthew would stop there and kiss her tenderly. The decoration remained suspended for all the decades of their marriage until Matthew died. Then Maggie took it down and threw it away, the memory of Matthew's lips on hers too painful to bear. But now she wished she had kept it or at least purchased one of those tiny ornaments on display in remembrance. But now they were gone.

It was all gone.

###

Tired of standing in one place, Susan came from behind the register and went over to a side table that was filled with last-minute gift ideas: boxes of ribbon candy, Santa pins, reindeer antlers for little ones to wear, and five little mistletoe clusters, each adorned with a tiny silver bell.

They reminded her of the first time Brandon had kissed her—two Christmases ago at a holiday party under a cluster of mistletoe. It wasn't the first time Susan had been kissed—at twenty-four, she had had her share of boyfriends—but somehow with Brandon it had been different, magical even. And after that, there was no looking back.

She picked up one of the little ornaments and shook it gently, holding back her tears at the sound, at the memory.

Then she gathered up the others and moved all five of them to the register counter, hoping to spark last-minute sales. Maybe, if there was still an ornament left at closing time, she'd buy it for the baby's nursery. Then she could show it to Brandon when he came home.

If he came home.

"May I help you?"

Denise turned and saw the girl standing there, her smock straining across her midsection.

"I need a toy," Denise told her. "My husband and I are on our way to a party, and we're supposed to bring a toy to donate for a kid in a shelter, but he forgot to tell me about it until now and —" Denise stopped, realizing she was on the verge of tears.

Was it the season? The display of items for children of all ages? Or was it the sight of this girl whose belly was so big and heavy that it was hard to believe she could even stand upright?

Without warning, waves of envy washed over Denise, so strong that she had to hold onto a shelf for balance. Why could *this* girl get pregnant and not her? The clerk appeared to be only in her twenties. She had lots of time ahead of her to have kids! But at best, Denise only had a few more years to go before the risks of having a baby in her forties outweighed the positives. "Geriatric pregnancy" or "advanced maternal age"—that's what it was called when an older woman was expecting. She'd read about it in one of the women's magazines at her gynecologist's office and was horrified to know that *she* would be in that category if she conceived and that there were so many things that could go wrong.

It was her fault. She *knew* that—no matter what the specialist had said. Jack had wanted them to have a baby right after they got married, but Denise had put it off. Had put *him* off. She didn't want to be tied down. She liked that they could go whenever and wherever they wanted without having to worry about dealing with the responsibility of a child.

"There's plenty of time for us to be parents," she had told him more than once. But then, once they made the decision to try, it was as though fate was punishing her for her selfishness, and she couldn't conceive. And she took it out on Jack, even though he wasn't to blame.

"How about this one?" asked the young clerk, picking up a snowman with a pink scarf around its neck. "If you squeeze it, it says 'Mama'," and she handed it to Denise. "I was thinking of buying one myself, but not until after the baby is born so I'd know what color bow to pick. Although I guess I could buy one with a yellow bow. We don't know if it's going to be a boy or a girl. Brandon—that's my husband—and I want to be surprised, so I told the doctor not to tell me. We'll find out together when the baby comes."

Just then, the register bell sounded. The clerk glanced toward the front of the store then back at Denise. "Well, if there's nothing you need…" But when Denise didn't answer, she added, "Just come up front when you're ready," before leaving.

Denise stood there, the snowman in her hands, not even noticing that the girl had gone. All she could think about was that *she* would never have to wait for nine long months to find out whether she was having a boy or girl. *She* would never hold her baby—Jack's baby—in her arms. *She* would never *have* a baby.

And if things didn't change—if *she* didn't change—a baby would not be the only thing she wouldn't have. She might not have Jack as well.

###

"Anything else?" asked the out-of-breath and pregnant cashier as she hurried back to the register. A very pregnant cashier, Maggie noticed, momentarily distracted from her memories.

"No, that's it," she answered, setting the cream on the counter. Then, seeing the display of mistletoe ornaments, she exclaimed, "Oh, there they are! I thought someone had bought them all. Here, I'll take one." She laid it next to the cream. "They remind me of... well, of someone special," she said, not wanting to say the words "my late husband" although surely by now she should be able to utter them without the rawness of the pain clutching at her.

"Well, it will make a very nice gift," the young woman said, wrapping it in red and green tissue paper. She took Maggie's money and gave the grocery bag to Maggie, who slipped it into her handbag. "Have a happy holiday!"

"The same to you," answered Maggie, all the while wondering how any holiday could be happy without Matthew by her side. Then once outside, Maggie found herself unable to go back to her empty house and instead turned toward the cemetery just a few blocks away.

It's so cold, she thought. Matthew hated the cold. They had always joked about moving somewhere warmer, Florida or Texas, but somehow they could never make the decision to do so. And now he was here for all eternity—alone until Maggie took her place beside him.

She brushed the snow from his gravestone, then said, "Matthew, Alix called. She wants me to come out there—she says for a visit, but I know she wants me to live with them. But I can't do it, Matthew! I can't leave the house where we were together for so long. I can't leave you!"

The tears came then, leaving frozen trails on her wrinkled cheeks. But when she reached into her handbag for a tissue, the small bag came out as well, sending the ornament tumbling to the ground where it lay half buried in the snow.

"Oh, no!" Maggie picked it up, shaking it free of the icy flakes. As she did so, the tiny bell rang. And just for a moment, Maggie felt a sense of comfort as though Matthew were kissing her one more time.

She really shouldn't leave her kid alone here, Jack thought shifting from one foot to the other while he waited for Denise. *The little guy looks sick, too. What was she thinking?*

"Santa's coming tonight," the boy said, moving closer to Jack. "He didn't come last year, but Mommy said it was because there were lots of other kids who needed stuff and he didn't have enough." He paused for a moment, then looked up at Jack as though to gauge if he could trust him with what he wanted to say. "But maybe this year, he might have a little extra and he can come to our house. But even if he doesn't, it's okay, Mommy said, because we have each other and lots of people are all alone."

"What's your name?" Jack asked, not because he really wanted to know but because he didn't know what else to say. He had no experience talking to kids.

"Joey. Well, really, it's Joseph, after my grandpa. He died last month. Mommy and I couldn't visit him very often because he lived so far away. Sometimes," and again Jack got the look from the child that meant he wanted to share something private, "I hear Mommy crying but I don't know what to do, so I just stay in my bed."

Jack wondered what he should say, or really, if there was anything he *could* say. But he knew how Joey felt, how helpless you feel when someone you love is in pain and there is nothing you can do or say. So, he settled for the one thing he could do and reached into his pocket for his wallet.

"Tell you what—why don't you take this," handing over a five-dollar bill, "and buy yourself a toy or something. Just in case Santa doesn't make it to your house after all."

The little boy's face lit up as he accepted the gift. "Thank you so much!" He hugged Jack, his arms barely reaching the tall man's waist, and said, "Merry Christmas!" before running off down the aisle. For a moment, Jack wondered if he had made a mistake. After all, the boy was supposed to stay there. But then he caught the cashier's eye, and she smiled.

"I'll keep an eye on him and let his mother know where he went," she said.

"Thanks," Jack said, adding, "Just let my wife know I'm outside, okay?" And without waiting for an answer, he left the store.

But even in the cold wind, he could feel the warmth of those small arms around his body.

###

Denise glanced at her watch. They were going to be late, very late. And it was all her fault. Still holding the snowman, she hurried to the front of the store and thrust it at the clerk, then looked around for her husband. But Jack wasn't there. Had he finally had enough of her anger and left her? *And* their marriage?

"Your husband wanted me to tell you he's outside," said the cashier as she rang up the purchase.

Denise let go of the breath she hadn't realized she was holding. Jack hadn't left her after all. There was still time to make things right, to tell him that she was sorry, to try to undo all the damage she had caused to their relationship. But how to start?

Just then, she noticed the small display of mistletoe ornaments. "I'll take one of those, too," she said. She wasn't sure why she was buying it or what Jack would think when she gave it to him, but she wanted to do it anyway. And even though it wasn't enough, it was at least a beginning.

###

Once at the toy aisle, Joey looked at the money the man had given him and for a minute thought about what he could get. A model car. Or maybe a new baseball. Or that fancy flashlight that had different colored lights. But as he looked at all the items, all he could see was his mother's sad face. Stuffing the money back in his pocket, he returned to the front of the store.

"I didn't know what to buy," he told the clerk. And then he saw them: the mistletoe ornaments with the shiny bells. "How much do they cost?" adding "It's for my mommy but I only have five dollars."

"I think that will be enough," she said with a smile. "And I can even wrap it in some pretty paper and tie a bow around it to make it look really special."

Joey picked the one he thought was the best and handed it to the cashier with his money, then watched anxiously for his mother. Then, just as the clerk handed him the package, he heard his mother's voice.

"Joey? Where are you?"

"Don't tell her!" he begged, stuffing the gift into his pocket.

She put her finger to her lips. "It's our secret!" she assured him.

He hurried back to stand by the door, hardly able to wait until he could give it to her.

Maybe it would make his mother happy, at least for a little while.

"Joey? Oh, there you are," Carol said in relief as she caught sight of her son waiting by the door. She smiled at the cashier. "Thanks for watching him," and then set the carton of juice, jar of peanut butter and loaf of day-old bread on the counter. Maybe there might be enough left to buy something small for Joey, too. But what? All the toys cost at least five dollars, and she didn't have that much extra.

A decoration maybe? And then she caught sight of the mistletoe ornaments, the ones she had seen before. She had looked for them again but thought they were all gone. But, no, they had only been moved.

She chose one and pushed it across the counter. "Put this in its own bag, please," she said softly, tipping her head toward her son.

The young girl smiled as she nodded and then rang up the items. "That will be fourteen dollars and fifty cents, please."

Carol stopped short. All she had was a ten-dollar bill. "I'm sorry. I mean, I don't have—"

But before she could finish, the cashier said, "Oh, my mistake. I forgot the holiday items are half price. Let me ring it up again." And before Carol could say anything, the young girl ran the items back through and said, "The correct total is nine dollars and ninety-two cents."

"Are you sure?" Carol asked, hardly believing her luck as she handed over the money.

"Yes indeed, and you have a wonderful Christmas!"

Carol smiled. "I will. We both will!" And then, taking Joey by the hand, she said, "Come on, honey. We have to catch the bus!"

But just outside the store he pulled at her to make her stop. "Wait, wait! I have something for you," and in the light from the streetlamp, he handed over the package. "Open it now, Mommy!"

Carol undid the bow and unfolded the tissue paper. The bell on the ornament glittered in the light.

"Merry Christmas, Mommy!" he shouted.

She started to laugh as she handed him his ornament. "Merry Christmas to you, too, sweetheart!"

###

Five minutes to closing time and Susan had never been so glad to see the end of her shift. Her feet hurt, her back hurt, and now her stomach was starting to ache, too. All she had left to do was walk through the aisles to make sure everyone was gone, and then she could start shutting down the store for the night.

But just as she reached the rear of the store, she heard the entrance door chime.

"We're closing in a few minutes," she called as she walked back up front. But there was no one in sight, just the last mistletoe ornament sitting on the counter.

"What's that doing there?" she said. "Hello, is anyone here?"

Then she gasped, a sudden pain catching her unawares. It wasn't like the baby's kick. It was different, stronger and sharper, and she grasped the counter until the pain eased up. She closed her eyes and took a few deep breaths, and then, when she opened them, saw a man's hand next to hers and felt an arm around her waist.

"Please, I need to—" but before she could finish, she heard him speak.

"You need to go to the hospital. Right now. And I'm going to be there with you, just like I promised."

Susan looked up, hardly daring to believe it might be true. But it was. It was her husband in his Army uniform, smiling down at her.

"I told you I'd be home in time." Brandon kissed her gently. "Come on, little mother. It's time for us to meet our Christmas baby!"

About the Author

Ohio-based Nancy Christie is the award-winning author of two short story collections, _Traveling Left of Center and Other Stories_ and _Peripheral Visions and Other Stories_ (published by Unsolicited Press), and three non-fiction books: _The Gifts of Change_ (Atria/Beyond Words) and _Rut-Busting Book for Writers_ and _Rut-Busting Book for Authors_ (both by Mill City Press). Her third short fiction collection, _Mistletoe Magic and Other Holiday Tales_, will be released by Unsolicited Press in 2023. Her debut novel, _Reinventing Rita_, will be released June 2023 by BookBaby. Her short stories have appeared in numerous literary publications including _The Saturday Evening Post, Commuter Lit, Goat's Milk Magazine, Ariel Chart, One Person's Trash, Two Cities Review, Talking River, Edify Fiction, Toasted Cheese, Wanderings, The Chaffin Journal_ and _Down in the Dirt_, among others, with several earning contest placements.

A member of the _American Society of Journalists and Authors (ASJA), Women's Fiction Writers Association (WFWA)_, and the _Florida Writers Association (FWA)_, Christie is the host of the _Living the Writing Life podcast_ and founder of the annual _"Celebrate Short Fiction" Day_. She also teaches _writing workshops_ at conferences, libraries and schools.

NANCY CHRISTIE

For more about Christie, visit her website (https://www.nancychristie.com/) & follow her on Facebook, Twitter, Instagram, Goodreads, LinkedIn and You Tube. To interview her or book her for a speaking engagement, book signing or other event, contact her via email at nancy@nancychristie.com or at 330-793-3675.

About the Press

Unsolicited Press is based out of Portland, Oregon, and focuses on the works of the unsung and underrepresented. As a womxn-owned, all-volunteer small publisher that doesn't worry about profits as much as championing exceptional literature, we have the privilege of partnering with authors skirting the fringes of the lit world. We've worked with emerging and award-winning authors such as Shann Ray, Amy Shimshon-Santo, Brook Bhagat, Kris Amos, and John W. Bateman.

Learn more at unsolicitedpress.com. Find us on Twitter and Instagram: @unsolicitedp.

Printed in the USA
CPSIA information can be obtained
at www.ICGtesting.com
CBHW030903201223
2784CB00004B/233